MARTIN MAGNUS ON VENUS

By the same author
in Dragon Books

MARTIN MAGNUS, PLANET ROVER

Copyright © William F. Temple, 1955

Martin Magnus on Venus
was first published in 1955 by
Frederick Muller Ltd.
This edition was published in 1970
by Mayflower Books Ltd.,
3, Upper James Street, London W.1.
It was printed in the U.K. by
C. Nicholls & Company Ltd.,
The Philips Park Press, Manchester

Martin Magnus
On Venus

William F. Temple

Contents

CHAPTER ONE

CRACK-UP

It was an exhilarating moment – also a fearful one. Cliff Page, apprentice space-pilot, fledgling member of the Special Investigation Department of the Scientific Bureau, laid his slightly trembling hands on the console central panel, realizing only too well that between them he was holding the lives of four people – one of them his.

It wasn't the first time he had taken over full control of a spaceship. Indeed, on the long flight back from Venus the skipper had once let him change the course of the *Archimedes*, then the largest atomic ship in existence. But in that case errors didn't much matter. Between Venus and Earth lay some twenty-six million miles of nothingness, and the *Archimedes* had more room to manoeuvre than an ant in St. Paul's Cathedral.

Now he was in the small lunar ship *Valier* – compared with the *Archimedes* a mere squib. There was another vital difference: the *Valier* was scarcely a thousand miles above the surface of the Moon and was dropping towards it at ever-increasing acceleration.

Already it was falling a whole mile every second.

That fall had to be checked so precisely that the *Valier* set its tail down on the hard lunar rock gently enough not to crumple its fins. It was tricky. A seasoned pilot would still rather make ten take-offs than one landing, even a lunar landing, which was one of the easiest.

For there was never an overplus of propellant to play with for landing.

The *Valier*-class atomic ships were ingeniously compact – but small. They were little more than a water tank, an atomic pile to turn that water to superheated steam and so jet the ship along by reaction to this sudden expansion, and a cramped cabin. The cabin contained the controls, the crew of two, and theoretical living space for three passengers. But Martin Magnus and Cliff Page, the only passengers on this trip, were finding only four a crowd.

The bulk of the water propellant had to be used up in overcoming the great gravitational pull of Earth. The remaining gallons were, again in theory, sufficient to cope with the welcoming clutch of the Moon, which pulled you towards it six times more slowly than Earth – but still in a hug of death if you hadn't the strength to resist it. According to the instruction manual of this class of ship, you should have not only enough water left for a comfortable landing, but afterwards still have sufficient for a hot bath – or, at least, a decent wash.

In actual fact, only pilots of the calibre of Magnus finished up on the Moon with more than a cupful of water in the tank.

Therefore, a landing always set everyone's nerves on edge – particularly those of the people in the ship.

If the pilot used too much water too soon, there would be none left for last-minute corrections. If he held back too much reserve, the landing speed would be too high and he'd crack up the ship – and likely break the occupants' necks.

He had to be right.

Another worry was getting – and keeping – the ship vertical during the descent. The heavy flywheels of the gyroscopes did the work for the pilot here – if he handled them surely. If not, he might ground the ship with it tilted at an angle too steep for the eight spidery shock-absorber legs to cope with. A ship crashing on to its side could easily dash a hole in its hull if it fell on a fang of rock – and even the seemingly smooth lunar Mares in places looked like cemeteries.

If the cabin were thus holed, out into the near-vacuum would rush the precious air, taking with it the last breath of the unhappy voyagers.

It seemed to Cliff Page, tremulous at the console, that all these considerations were trying to force themselves upon his attention at once. Additionally, he was aware of the regard of the other three men – including Martin Magnus's, although Magnus didn't appear to be regarding anything except his finger-nails.

The testing time had come.

He tried to forget everything but the trembling needles on the dials and the bright green radar pictures on the screens in an arc before him. One needed to be Argus-eyed to watch them all at once.

Falling too fast, said the altimeter. Gently, Cliff turned a knob and the first gouts of atomized water went shooting downwards. Just as gently, he himself sank towards the floor, for, like the others, he had been floating in a state of free fall. As his feet grounded a slight sensation of weight returned.

Still too fast, said the altimeter. Cliff increased the speed of the propellant pumps. At once the floor seemed to start rising, like that of a lift. His knees buckled. He had to clutch at the console for support.

The needle of the propellant gauge swung wildly towards the red danger mark. It conveyed agitatedly that the precious water was being squandered.

Cliff slowed the pumps, and the sweat broke on his forehead.

Then the vertical indicator started to tilt slowly towards the right. He knew what had happened. His too savage braking had disturbed the axes of the two gyros. The ship was being carried off balance.

In a panic, he glanced desperately at Martin Magnus. That lanky young man was leaning against the curved wall, wedging himself by one bony shoulder under a bracket, and apparently having difficulty with a piece of grime beneath his thumb-nail. He was silently preoccupied. Cliff was relieved. It couldn't be so bad. For when things looked grim, Magnus had a way of bursting into song.

Bill, the pilot-navigator (who'd had small chance to practise his craft on this trip, for Cliff was a keen learner), and Rodney, the engineer, watched impassively. But Cliff imagined their faces were a trifle paler than before. Perhaps it was only the increasing glare of the moonlight.

Cliff juggled with the Gyro "A" and Gyro "B" controls, while trying to watch also the altimeter and the propellant gauge. Presently, the vertical indicator started a slow backward swing, and he managed to get it on the mark and hold it there. For a brief space he felt the glow of a helmsman who'd got the compass back in line and had it under control, despite a storm. The propellant stream was running steadily now, too, and there was still a satisfactory amount in hand.

He felt safe enough to take a peep at the ordinary TV screen, recording the view from the camera set in a blister on the ship's hull. About five hundred square miles of Moon was visible, looking like a sheet of crumpled white paper with black ink blots scattered over it. The blots were the shadows of minor eminences and small craters, for this was the Mare Nubium, one of the flatter regions of the Moon. They grew slowly larger as he watched, moving out towards the edges of the screen.

The ship was still descending rather too fast, but almost nonchalantly now he thickened the jet stream.

Before glancing away from the screen he discerned three glittering points, clustered together. Not far from them was a short bright line. The points were the woven glass filament domes of Lunar Base Two. The line was the foreshortened aspect of the silvered hull of *Archimedes II*, the great new atomic ship which was to repeat the exploit of its predecessor, the ship *Archimedes*, and make the long voyage to Venus.

A much bigger shining line, which lay some miles from them, was one of Tycho's streaks.

Then his attention was back on the dials. He found it easier to watch them all now. It was just a question of knowing what to look for. He reminded himself that all things came with practice. It looked as though he had the makings of a pretty good space-pilot after all.

This good opinion held until he happened to glance casually at one screen he should have watched earlier. It was that of the horizontal radar scanner, directed towards Base Two. The three domes showed up quite clearly on it. Eventually, the ship should come to rest with them arranged neatly along the horizon, for the official landing perimeter was a circle four miles in diameter, with the Base at the centre. This was for a good reason. The Moon's horizon, from any spot in flat country is no more than two miles distance. There being no lunar Heaviside Layer to reflect radio waves over that horizon, it was necessary for a ship to remain in direct line of sight with the Base if radio contact with it were desired.

Out in space the *Valier* had been in radio communication with the Base. But, following the recognized procedure, they had both shut down the moment the *Valier* prepared to land. It was dangerous to distract a pilot's attention with radio messages during the last critical operations. Then communication would be opened up again directly after the ship landed.

So Cliff's new-found self-esteem collapsed pitifully when he saw on the horizontal scanner screen the domes of Base Two sinking *below* the horizon. It meant that he was setting the *Valier* down way outside the perimeter, outside the region of radio contact.

Worse – as he saw now from the TV screen – he was dropping the ship into the reaching black shadow of a tall rock-mound which stood on the great plain.

And then Magnus, regarding him from under lowered brows, began to hum. Magnus, who loved music but had the world's worst singing voice, was a mile off key, and the tune was only just recognizable. It was "Down Among the Dead Men."

10

Bill and Rodney both had a little more colour in their cheeks now. It was disturbing that the colour appeared to be green.

Clifford Page, space-pilot, gave place to Clifford Page, jelly-fish. He felt very small, and everything about him seemed much too big. Every ounce of the hundred-ton ship seemed to be weighing on his shoulders. Yet the *Valier* itself was but a mote compared with the great world of rock it was about to impinge upon.

The inertia of the heavy flywheels when they were at the wrong angle had driven the ship laterally off course. He had forgotten to allow for and correct that. Now he would have to land where he could, and the TV screen which should have pictured the nearing ground showed only the blackness of shadow. He must land blind, by meter indications only.

He set his teeth. Greenhorn pilot notwithstanding, he was still a S.I.D. man, and that meant he had to fight to the last. He concentrated upon the illuminated meters as though it were a matter of life and death because – it was.

Afterwards, he didn't know how he'd done it. Whether it had been the blossoming of an inborn piloting instinct or just a case of pure luck.

The *Valier* landed on the cracked lunar surface, sprang once like a huge insect, rocked a bit, then was still. The occupants began to breathe normally again.

Magnus was the first to speak. "I've known worse lunar landings. Why, I doubt if I've bitten even halfway through my tongue!"

Bill said, with the heartiness of relief: "Well done, young 'un! It was better than *my* first landing. They can still see the dent I made from Mount Palomar."

Rodney looked surprised to find he was still alive, and could manage no more than a weak grin and a wink that was meant to be encouraging.

Cliff wiped his face with his sleeve. His hands were still shaking and his heart was thumping away to a quick-step rhythm.

"Sorry I missed the target by so much. I didn't even score an inner."

"The magpie will do," said Magnus, biting at a wafer of gum. "Don't worry, Cliff, the Base radar trackers will have marked our general direction. The tractor will have to come a bit farther for us, that's all."

Bouncing slightly under the weak gravitation, Cliff went over to a porthole. He peered through. One edge of the pyramid of shadow which enfolded the ship was sharply defined on the

11

ground, a quarter of a mile away. Sunlight and shadow lay side by side there in absolute contrast. Beyond, the brilliantly lit rock layer rose and fell in shallow undulations to the horizon, like a sea with a slight swell on it frozen in its motion. Except overhead, the glare dimmed the stars. Earth was not visible from this side of the ship.

How many miles away over that horizon lay Base Two? Perhaps ten. Perhaps less.

"Do you think they'll spot us in this shadow, Magnus?" Cliff asked.

Magnus shrugged. "It doesn't matter. We'll be able to see *them*. Directly the tractor shoves its nose over the horizon we'll radio the crew and tell 'em where we are." He stuck the remainder of the wafer in his mouth and added indistinctly: "Let's get the armour ready."

Armour was the collective term for lunar spacesuits, which were weighty metallic things, silvered on the outside to reflect the sun's killing heat, insulated on the inside to retain the body's warmth. There was the thinnest of atmospheres on the Moon, much too thin to mitigate by much the blinding ultra-violet rays or the tissue-destroying cosmic rays. The suits had to be heavy to furnish complete protection. It would be necessary to wear them while transferring from the ship to the tractor.

Magnus reached for his suit but never touched it. For suddenly, inexplicably, he was hovering a foot or more above the floor. Then he was falling, but he couldn't touch the floor again because it also was falling, falling away beneath him. His confusion was only part of the whole. Cliff and the other two were in the same predicament. He and they and the *Valier* were falling together – into the Moon's mysterious depths.

The fluorescent lighting flickered like a signal lamp, but kept alive.

A few seconds later, they all hit the floor with a jolt and this time Magnus did bite his tongue. The ship heeled over and fell on its side, and the wall became the floor and again they hit it together and rolled hurtfully into each other, while the spacesuits danced on their hooks, adding their jangling to the general din. Cliff cushioned Magnus's much too sharp elbow with his nose and the tears at once came streaming from his eyes.

And then the ship was falling again, but this time very slowly, with a sickening rocking motion that kept its passengers still rolling, though more gently, on the curved wall that was the floor.

This lasted but a minute, It ended, and everyone was physically at rest, though their brains seemed to be spinning.

Martin Magnus pushed himself up on to his knees. Dazedly, he retrieved the blob of chewing gum from the wall and resumed masticating it. The others sat up and regarded one another blearily. None spoke. They seemed to be awaiting an official announcement about what had happened. Magnus made an obvious show of counting heads. "Four," he said. "We're all here. The question is – where is here?"

Cliff said, like someone waking from a dream: "I think we've fallen through the lunar crust."

"Obviously," said Magnus. He crawled up the concave slope to a porthole and looked through. He peered for a while and then beckoned to Cliff. Cliff pulled himself together and climbed up alongside him.

"What do you make of that?" asked Magnus, granting him the point of view. Cliff stared hard through the porthole. It was inky black outside except for the pale beam of the cabin's light reaching past his head into the gloom. He saw nothing but that at first, but gradually he became aware of what appeared to be specks of dust floating in the beam.

"We seem to have kicked up a lot of dust," he said. "I don't wonder."

Magnus sighed. "The lunar atmosphere is too thin to support even dust. You should know that, Cliff. Bill, Rod – what do you gather from this?"

Feeling a little nettled, Cliff relinquished his place to the other two. And even while they were looking and wondering the solution occurred to him. He snapped his fingers. "We're under water!" he exclaimed. "Those specks are the plankton the decapods fed upon."

On his last – which was also his first – trip to the Moon he and Magnus had encountered some intelligent ten-tentacled creatures they had named the "decapods" – a few long-lived survivors of an ancient race. These beings could live in or out of water, although they favoured the latter element. Below the ground in certain areas around Base Two were some systems of linked caverns, and they had formed the whole world for the decapods.

The creatures knew nothing of Earth until the Earthmen came and began pumping the water from the caverns because they needed it for spaceship propellant. This had led to conflict between men and decapods but, thanks to Magnus, the star investigator for the S.I.D., an amicable settlement was reached: the

13

dwindling decapod race was taken entire to Earth and given the freedom of its seas in exchange for the water remaining in their little world below the Moon. For it was far easier to transport a few creatures to Earth than to carry hundreds of thousands of tons of water to the near-arid Moon.

The decapods, who knew elementary chemistry at least, had kept their caves full of oxygen which they, like all known creatures, needed to breathe to live. But now they had left the Moon. Nothing more than the extremely tenuous lunar atmosphere remained in the caves. It was sufficient to support simple fungi and even, it appeared now, the specks of life, half animal, half vegetable, which drifted in the subterranean sea and had formed part of the decapods' diet.

No one had charted the sea, but according to the decapods the caverns were of limited extent. The water was salty and very cold – it was kept just a little above freezing point by the Moon's inner fires, which were by no means dead, as once supposed. It varied in depth but in places reached around fifty fathoms.

Bill said: "I'm sure you're right, Cliff. I wonder how deep under we are?"

"We're on the bottom – we've stopped rolling," said Magnus. "My guess is that we floated for a bit while the water poured in through the main vent and refilled the propellant tank. We're fuelled up again, boys! All we've got to do is press the firing button and off we go."

Rodney, who'd not yet learned when to take Magnus seriously and when not to, exclaimed: "Of course! What are we worrying about? Let's go."

Bill, who was brighter, said: "Pinhead! He's kidding. The ship's lying on its side. We'd shoot straight into the wall."

"That would certainly end our worries," said Magnus, dryly. "It's a pity we didn't finish up on our tail, pointing up at the hole we fell through."

"There wasn't any hole there to begin with," said Cliff. "I *would* have to set her down on a thin part of the crust, which couldn't stand up to the weight of the ship for long."

Magnus stroked his beak of a nose thoughtfully. "I'm worried about that hole. I don't suppose it's much wider across than the ship's diameter. And that makes it a pretty small black hole in a black shadow. It won't exactly be shriekingly obvious when the tractor comes looking for us. They may miss it altogether, and then we'd be sunk – doubly. Our air supply isn't going to last for ever: we've used the bulk of it on the trip. Or they mightn't miss it

14

at all. They might run straight into it – and then they'd be sunk too. On top of us. Remember, they'll be watching for the *Valier*, not a hole in the ground."

"Shan't we be able to warn them by radio?" asked Rodney.

"Gosh, when I called you a pinhead it seems I was complimenting you," said Bill, sarcastically. "Do I have to remind you that we're both underwater and underground? Our radio signals won't get any farther than you could throw them by hand – they'll never reach the tractor."

"That sounds reasonable," Rodney admitted, "but a mite discouraging. You might say we're in a spot."

"Cheer up," said Magnus. "Now, I remember piloting an early model of one of these craft in my youth. I took off nicely, Moonbound. I was quite ten miles on the way when the vent split and the ship started to act like a pin-wheel. I didn't seem to be getting anywhere but dizzy, so I shut off the power, and soon we began to fall back in a nice curve towards the Atlantic. But, as you chaps know, there's a drill for that sort of thing."

Bill and Rodney knew, and just nodded, but Cliff was eager to air his hard-won space knowledge, and jumped in: "You pulled the emergency separation lever."

"I certainly did," said Magnus. For the small cabin of the *Valier*-class ship was lightly built and detachable from the main body, as – especially in the early days – sometimes engineering defects caused spaceships to fall back to Earth. To this day they were launched on a path that would take them as soon as possible over the open sea just in case of such emergencies. The bulk of the ship, with its heavy tank, atomic reactor and shielding, would be jettisoned into the sea. The cabin would follow more slowly, swinging on a series of automatically opened parachutes. Being light and air-filled, it would float on the waves, and the space-travellers would have to endure nothing worse than sea-sickness until the rescue ship reached them.

Magnus reached for the separation lever "We're going to pop to the surface like an air-bubble. Hold on, lads."

He gave a strong heave on the lever, for it was not a thing to be moved accidentally, and the mechanism was designedly stiff. And went flying backwards under his own impetus: the lever was as free as the joy-stick of an aeroplane. He sat up, looking almost as surprised as the others. "Forgot to hold on myself," he muttered.

Bill examined the lever. It waggled like a loose tooth. "I tested

15

it myself before take-off," he said. "Something must have broken in that last fall."

Cliff felt miserable and guilty. "You've got me to thank for everything –"

"Pipe down," said Magnus. "It's nobody's fault – except the designers'. They should have used thicker cable. It's snapped somewhere below the floor where we can't get at it. I wish someone had thought up an emergency release for the emergency release. We're still anchored. The maddening part about it is that I'm sure the whole ship would float – though maybe only just – if the darned water tank hadn't filled again. Let's put our thinking caps on. There must be a way out."

Cliff asked almost at once: "Can that broken cable be reached from outside?"

"No," said Magnus. "You can't do a thing outside about releasing the cabin, short of using dynamite. Anyway, how the devil can you get outside?"

Cliff pointed to the spacesuits. "In one of those. It'll be as good as any diving suit."

"H'm." Magnus chewed thoughtfully, then removed the detachable leaden soles (which were to help the wearer to walk normally under the weak gravitation) from the feet of the nearest suit. He weighed them in his hands, then shook his head. "Even with these off, the suit's far too heavy to surface in. You could promenade around the sea-bottom until your air-cylinders were empty. Then you'd only have to come back in here, bringing an airlock full of water with you. That won't help any."

"I don't know," said Cliff. "There's a chance the sea-bottom may slope up to a ledge or something and I could walk – or climb – up to it."

"Perhaps," said Magnus. "But from what I remember of these caves, the walls are pretty sheer everywhere. And as they meet overhead, how could you hope to get out?"

"That's a bridge that can wait till I reach it."

"Too risky," said Magnus, shaking his head.

"That's fine talk, coming from you," said Cliff, surprised.

"I've a better idea," said Magnus. He opened a compartment and dragged from it a rolled-up collapsible raft of tough fabric. "I'd forgotten one or two items we have on board."

The raft was also emergency gear. The crew were meant to take to it should the cabin spring a leak and begin to founder in the sea. It was rolled around a thin cylinder of highly compressed air, which would inflate the raft at the touch of a spring button.

16

"This will carry you to the surface," said Magnus.

"Can't it take us all up?"

"No, Cliff. It'll bear three men without spacesuits – but only one with. I don't think the roof of this cave can be very far above the surface – it seemed to me that we fell only a short distance. Standing on the raft, you may be able to reach the lip of the hole with this."

He produced from the same compartment a short telescopic ladder of aluminium with a grip-hook at one end. It was an implement used by lunar prospectors when negotiating awkward climbs on the mountains, and was part of the small cargo of replacements for Base Two the *Valier* was carrying.

Cliff took these things. He checked that the oar was securely strapped to the raft, but he seemed to be debating something within his mind. He looked round at Bill and Rodney, then back to Magnus.

"I think we'd better draw lots for this job," he said. "Frankly, I don't see how the ship is going to be raised. The tractor doesn't carry the tackle to do it. It might take days. . . . And there isn't a day's air supply left. I can't just get out of here on the only raft and leave you fellows here like – like people trapped in a submarine. After all, I'm to blame for landing you in this mess –"

"Here's that theme song again," said Magnus. "Okay, you got us here. Now, off you go and get us out of here."

"Personally," said Rodney, "I'd rather stay here and take my chance. There's still more air here than you have in your cylinders, Cliff. If you don't make the tractor within a few hours, I shouldn't like to change places with you."

"That's right," said Bill. "You worry about us, Cliff, and we'll worry about you."

Cliff hesitated, and then: "All right, I'll go. Good luck, boys."

They assisted him into the spacesuit and added a large handtorch to his burdens. They pushed him into the air-lock and, with a farewell pat on his helmet, shut the door on him. Clutching the raft, the ladder, and the torch, he was very cramped in there, and the fact that the chamber was lying at an acute tilt added nothing to his comfort.

He opened the small vents in the outer door which normally allowed the passage of air in one direction or the other. This time water came squirting in and soon filled the chamber save for a pocket of air trapped at the top – and this rushed out in a great bubble when he pushed open the outer door.

He stepped over the rim and dropped a few feet to the hard

17

floor of the underground sea. It wasn't wholly dark – the ship's portholes cast some light on the surroundings, which were little but water and rock.

Holding tightly with metal fingers to the cordage of the raft, he pressed the spring button. The raft writhed and grew rapidly, like some weird monster coming into being, and he felt the upward tug of it. It was insistent, but gentle – too gentle, he feared. The weight of the suit was a terrible drag on the raft. It was touch and go whether there was enough buoyancy to lift him. He was considering taking the long chance of jettisoning the ladder, hoping it would make just the difference, when he noticed the beam from one porthole seem slowly to travel down his upreaching arms. But the ship couldn't move, so it meant that he was rising – at last.

The motion was so slow and the light so poor, and being unable to feel the water about him, he wasn't aware of the actual moment when he did break surface. But when he switched on his torch, he found his head was above water, and he was hanging on to the side of a raft which was floating on an ice-calm expanse. Clumsily, he clambered on to the top-side, which yielded to his weight. It was like squatting in the hollow of a big soft cushion.

There was a raggedly circular hole in the roof above, its shape defined by the stars thick in the black sky, as if they'd crowded together to look in on him curiously.

He explored the walls briefly by torchlight. It could show him only a small round patch at a time, but he could see the fungi still clinging to them. He experimented by switching off the torch, and found the plants had retained their dim luminosity. Once his eyes had grown accustomed to it, this phosphorescence, added to the starlight, was preferable to the torch, which lit a small area brightly but made the rest darker, almost invisible, by contrast. So he hung the torch from a waist-clip, deciding to do without it.

The cave was long and narrow, and he couldn't see the far ends of it. The only apparent way out was the way they had come in – through the hole in the roof.

He stood up, uncertainly poised on the raft, and extended the telescopic ladder to its limit, which was twelve feet. He reached up with it as high as he could. Infuriatingly, the grip-hook bobbed about only a few inches beneath the nethermost edge of the hole. It was difficult to jump, as the raft tended to sink beneath his feet when he moved suddenly.

However, he managed one undignified hop. The hook scraped pieces from the side of the hole but didn't catch. He fell back awkwardly on to the raft, which slid across the water, unbalancing

18

him altogether. He landed on his side and would have rolled into the water if he hadn't caught the cordage in time.

He lay on his back, trembling a little at the escape. It would be silly to try that again. If he did fall into the water he would sink at once, and there would be no coming up again.

As he rested there, looking up, he noticed a long crack in the roof which sprang from the edge of the hole and obviously had been caused by it. It widened, narrowed, and widened again, and at one point about a dozen yards away it looked perhaps wide enough to get through – if he could reach it. And even that might be possible, for the roof sloped gently downwards from the central hole.

He got to his knees, unstrapped the oar, and paddled the raft along, following the direction of the crack. He was looking up at it intently all the time, and so was taken by surprise when the raft bumped into something and stopped suddenly.

Whatever it was, it couldn't be very obvious, else he would have noticed it before. He shone the neglected torch on the front of the raft. It was nudging against a smooth black hump, which showed only a few inches above the icy water and looked like the back of a motionless and exceptionally large seal. Yet it hadn't reacted to the impact of the raft.

Perhaps it was only a rock. He prodded it with the end of the ladder, and then with his fingers. It was hard. His imagination pictured it as the armour of an enormous crab or turtle. But still it didn't stir, and he gathered the courage to fumble around it, his hands reaching below the water level. Presently, they encountered a jagged edge. His wonder grew as he felt along it. The thing was only a shell, about an inch thick. Could this be a natural growth, the broken egg-shell of some huge and unknown lunar sea creature?

Gingerly, despite his metal gloves, he reached into it and continued to feel about. When his arm was under to the shoulder, his fingers became entangled in something that might have been tough seaweed. He tugged at it, breaking a handful away, and pulled it out for inspection by torchlight.

It looked like a tangle of thin wire, but still might have been some strange marine plant – except for one thing. From two strands of the stuff there dangled a disc, like a small medal, gleaming in the light. He held it close to his face-plate, peering. One side was blank. The other, transparent, glassy, showed the face of a meter dial, its needle bent as if by some sudden shock.

He could see the graduations, but the figures or letters standing

19

beside them were too tiny to read through the slightly distorting quartz of his face-plate.

Nevertheless, they told him something with startling clarity: this broken casing he had stumbled upon, whatever it was and whatever it contained, had been built by someone with intelligence and technical skill. And it wasn't the decapods, for their tools were primitive and clumsy, and they could never, even if they had the knowledge, have fashioned anything so delicate as this.

Much as he would have liked to continue investigating, there were more pressing things to attend to. His own life and the lives of the trio trapped under this dark water depended upon the speed and effectiveness of his actions.

Carefully he placed the meter and its trailing appendages in the sample box attached to his suit, and stood up to resume fishing at the roof with the ladder. The hook kept tapping against the side of the wide portion of the crack, but failed to lodge. He could see its curved shape dark against the bright star sprinkle, like a metal snake, striking unavailingly.

His arms began to ache. Another few inches of elevation were still needed. He took a deep breath and stepped cautiously from the raft on to the black hump. It rocked a little and his feet slid about on the smooth convex surface, sending his heart into his mouth. But he managed to regain his equilibrium.

Once more he thrust the top of the ladder up into the crack. The hook inched over the top edge, out on the bleak lunar surface, naked to the stars. He put most of his weight on the ladder, testing it. It held. He put a foot determinedly on the lowest rung and began to climb as carefully as a circus acrobat.

The weak gravity helped a lot, but each step was something of an effort, probably because of his tenseness. Suppose the edge flaked away some more?

At last the fungus-covered roof passed slowly below his eye-level, and then he was looking along the ground, across the shadow towards the sunlit horizon. All relief now, he began to transfer his weight from the ladder on to that ground. He was too hasty and clumsy. He jarred the hook and it slid clean off the rim. He was left, leaning awkwardly and far from securely on his elbows, his feet dangling still in the cavern, while the ladder fell with a silent splash into the water twenty feet below.

And while he hung there, every nerve quivering, he saw a distant flash near the horizon. He had seen the like before. It was the sun catching the plastic hood of a lunar tractor as it turned.

The tractor from Base Two was coming. He strained to see clearly through the face-plate, and perceived the vehicle coming at an angle across the plain. It was an angle which would take it well away from the shadow in which he lay. Presumably it had turned to avoid the shadow, its occupants having observed that no spaceship stood there.

It would pass by and ramble perhaps many miles away over the next horizon, still searching long after he and Magnus, Bill and Rodney had died from suffocation.

Fear gave him strength. He heaved himself out of the crack and stood on its brink, waving his tired arms. It was completely useless to call out, but he found himself doing so, deafening himself in his helmet.

But the tractor crew were looking for a tall ship, not a man. Their eyes were on the distances. Small chance of them spotting him in this deep shadow, semaphore as he may. He would have to run out into the sunlight, where the sun would gleam on his silvered suit and perhaps mark him for them.

The nearest edge of the shadow was still a quarter of a mile away, and by the time he reached it the odds were that the tractor would have gone too far away in the wrong direction.

Nevertheless, he began to run with all his might. It was a queer bounding progression. Without the leaden soles, the suit lacked balance and was disconcertingly top-heavy. He had little control over his frantic feet. He stumbled when he landed at the end of each hop, and already he was beginning to gasp with anxiety and exhaustion.

The tractor rolled steadily on towards his left. Soon he found he was veering to chase it – and it was moving much faster than he. But he kept on.

The frontier of shadow and sunlight was still dishearteningly distant when he found himself sinking, first ankle-deep, then knee-deep, in a pan of fine volcanic dust. It was like a patch of quicksand. He attempted to turn and struggle back, and all at once the dust was around his thighs, impeding him so that he couldn't move either way.

Despairing, the sweat trickling into his eyes, he watched the tractor bowling merrily away over the endless reaches of the Mare Nubium, taking the last shred of his hope with it.

CHAPTER TWO

WHAT MAGNUS FOUND

From his fixed position Cliff could see Earth, big in the sky. The shadow of the night side had eaten away a whole quarter of it, including half the Americas. He could see the pale glow of moonlight over Mexico – the sunlight rebounding from the harsh desert around him was leaping across space to illumine the harsh desert there.

In a moment of weakness and self-pity he wished he could leap with it, back to the safety of his own world.

But was it so safe? There were rattlesnakes in those Mexican deserts and quicksands too, and a man could become just as lost and helpless there as he was here, and die, if not of suffocation, then of thirst.

Indeed, a desperate battle was going on all over Earth to save a much too large population from starvation. Attempts to reclaim the deserts of Mexico for agriculture would be made in time, as they were being made now in the Sahara and Gobi and in central Australia. Even the sea-beds were being sown with edible plants, and the seas themselves made to support plankton farms. The Scientific Bureau worked tirelessly on all these projects on Earth and on others across space.

For already man was reaching out to the nearer planets, seeking living room and food-growing areas. There were small colonies fighting to live in the deserts of Mars. The first landing on Venus had been made – by Cliff himself, in company with Magnus. It had been a very brief stay. The pair had been driven off by a kind of gas attack by some unseen, mysterious and most inhospitable inhabitants, who dwelt in the depths of a lake. Nothing except the shores of that lake had yet been explored on Venus, where the perpetual clouds reached down to ground-level and hid no Earthman knew what.

Now the couple had come to the Moon to join the second expedition to that misty planet. But as things had turned out, reflected Cliff miserably, it would seem that to Magnus and himself, at least, the secrets of Venus would remain forever unrevealed.

Truly this universe was a dangerous place, be one on Earth, the Moon, Venus or Mars.

All this passed through his mind as he watched the tractor dwindling away – beetle-sized now – in the distance.

Well, there it was. Exit Clifford Page. Short as his period of service for the Scientific Bureau had been, no one could deny he'd made the most of it. It was still something to have been a torch-bearer for civilization....

Torch-bearer! Belatedly, he remembered: he was literally just that. What a dim-wit he was not to have thought of it before!

He snatched the torch from his waist-clip and directed it after the disappearing tractor. He gave three short flashes, three long ones, then three short again, and kept repeating that group: the morse SOS signal had never gone out of use.

Probably he had left it too late now. If he had thought of it when the tractor was at its nearest, there would have been an excellent chance of someone seeing his flashes, for, weak as they were compared with the sunlight, they would have shown up distinctly against the velvety black pall of shadow lying over him.

There was still, even now, the chance of a keen-eyed searcher happening to glance backwards, for the tractor's translucent hood gave an all-round view.

Flash, flash, flash ... flash, flash, flash ... flash, flash, flash ...

Then he cried aloud with excitement, for the tractor was turning round. And now it was coming back towards him. But he kept on flashing, to make really sure.

On it came, caterpillar treads whirring round, reaching close to forty miles an hour, its top speed. Soon, through that thin dustless atmosphere he could see the two occupants within the bulge of the plastic hood. The tractor slowed when it reached the verge of the shadow, and suddenly its headlamps shot twin beams through the darkness. Then a spotlight came on, and when its light touched him he ceased signalling.

It was a bit unnerving to see a dim but huge monster, with three bright eyes, lumbering directly towards him and he unable to move. It made no detectable sound in the near-vacuum but the ground trembled at its approach.

However, in the spotlight's shaft his suit shone like that of a fairy prince, so there should be no danger of his being run down by accident.

The tractor proceeded carefully, avoiding the worst of the rock-fangs and cracks, but however it dipped and swayed, its spotlight remained on Cliff unswervingly. Whoever was handling it was certainly efficient at the job. The thing stopped with its forepart protruding over the edge of the dust bowl but still some yards from Cliff. Then it jerked forward another few yards, sinking slowly in the dust.

Frantically, Cliff waved it to a stop. Although tractors could negotiate most dust bowls, this particular pan was a lot stickier than the average, and the tractor would surely get bogged if it came any farther. Even so, it had reached to within six feet of him.

But Cliff's arms were nowhere near six feet long, and he was resigning himself to wait while one of the inmates struggled into a spacesuit and came out to his rescue when the "buffer" on the front of the vehicle (whose real job was to press the automatic door release of the airlocks at Base Two) pushed itself out towards him on its long thin pole. Obviously, someone in the tractor was a quick thinker.

He clung to the buffer with both hands, and at once the tractor went into reverse, dragging him out of his pit like a winkle on a pin. It was undignified, but freedom regained was a most pleasant feeling. The tractor deposited him at the bowl's edge. He picked himself up and went round to the airlock in the side of the tractor. The door was already opening, automatically.

The former chief at Base Two, Smith, had been recalled to Earth for what the Scientific Bureau termed "gross inefficiency." They had, Cliff had heard, replaced him with a man named Breen, of whom Cliff knew nothing except his reputation for being a live wire. Certainly, Cliff thought as he climbed into the lock, Breen had smartened up the tractor crews, at least, on his staff.

He waited in the lock until the air pressure was equal to that in the body of the tractor and then stumbled awkwardly into the inner compartment. He began fumbling to release the fastenings of his helmet.

Then someone pulled his head down and forward and peered in at him through the face-plate as though he were a fish in an aquarium. He resented this rather brusque treatment, but took it to be a bit of fooling, if ill-timed, and managed to grin at the face studying his. But there was no grin in response.

The stranger's face was small, pinched, sharp, and thick with freckles. He had a ginger moustache, waxed to points, and ginger hair brushed straight back and greased to hold it there. He might have been thirty – or forty. His eyes were yellowy-brown. They were open wide, as if he were amazed at the sight of Cliff. Then suddenly they narrowed and dexterously he unfastened Cliff's helmet and lifted it off.

"Thanks, Ginger," said Cliff, and took a deep and grateful

24

breath of air that wasn't, for a change, humid with his own moisture.

The man, who was small, opened his eyes wide again. He looked incredulous.

"My name is Breen. I am the chief at Two. You will address me as 'sir'."

Like his nose and chin, his tone was sharp, and his words were precisely articulated in every syllable. His whole attitude said, in effect: "I am making myself clear the first time so that you won't need telling a second time – or if you do, then heaven help you, for I do not suffer fools gladly."

Cliff was at once both irritated and interested. Irritated, because he disliked martinets. Interested, because if ever they got Martin Magnus out of his present predicament, then there was bound to be a head-on clash between him and Breen. For to Magnus, officiousness was like a red rag to a bull. The real boss on the Moon was the Commandant of Base One, who managed to be both efficient and fairly easy-going, and yet often he and Magnus had crossed swords.

"I'm sorry, sir," said Cliff, emphasizing the "sir" and making it plain from his expression that he was anything but sorry. He caught the eye of the driver, who winked solemnly at him.

Breen grunted. "Are you Magnus or Page?"

"Page, sir. I – "

"You don't have to tell me. I know who you are. You're the new young S.I.D. man, Magnus's assistant. I also know another thing."

"What's that, sir?"

"You're improperly dressed, man. Where are your lead soles? Lunar spacesuits are designed to be worn complete. There's a reason for every part of the equipment, including the soles. We may be on the Moon, we may be a quarter of a million miles from anywhere, but there's still a standard to maintain and, by heaven, my men will keep up to the mark."

"I'm sure *they* will, sir." This time Cliff threw the emphasis on "they." "My soles happen to be in the *Valier*, and that's – "

"Another thing," interrupted Breen. "Each suit is fitted with a radio. Why didn't you employ it? Luckily for you I'm a man who keeps my eyes open." (He opened them widely again as he said this.) "Anyone else mightn't have noticed your feeble torch signals."

Cliff, who was bursting to tell of the *Valier's* present situation, was nettled by this untimely pin-pricking. He said shortly: "I was

25

aware of the set but not of the tractor's wave-length. The last time I was here the tractor frequencies were changed at least twice. You were in view for such a short time – "

"You still had time to search round the dial for me," snapped Breen. "I was calling regularly every fifteen seconds."

"I wasn't sure of that, sir – I couldn't count on it. I thought it better to risk attracting your attention visually. I may have been wrong – "

"Of course you were wrong, Page. Again, why did you S.I.D. men stand by and let the fool of a pilot land the ship outside the perimeter? Isn't it your job to keep an eye on things like that?"

Cliff's heart sank to the level where his lead soles should have been. "It wasn't the pilot, sir. It was me. I – er – it was my first landing."

Breen's eyes looked in danger of popping from their sockets. He breathed hard.

"All right," he said, dangerously quietly and still very precisely, "we'll postpone the question of how you came to be piloting the ship, or even why you made such a mess of it. The pressing question is where is the ship now?"

"I've been trying to tell you," Cliff protested. "It's down there, somewhere." He pointed, and added: "Under water."

And then, of course, he had to endure the trial of explaining that.

When Breen had regained a precarious control of his eyes and breathing functions, he said: "I'm not moving this tractor an inch nearer that cavern – I don't want it too to be lost." He pulled from a locker a rolled ladder fashioned from a special plastic which remained strong and flexible at extreme temperatures. "You can carry that," he said to Cliff. "Tune your set to three hundred megacycles."

While Cliff busied himself, Breen donned his spacesuit. It was pint-sized and obviously had been made especially for him. A large letter "B" in black metal was inlaid both on his breastplate and back-plate. In the case of a normal suit it would have been useful for identification, for a group of people in spacesuits all look very much alike. But it was comically unnecessary on Breen's little suit, which alone would have distinguished him anywhere. It made him look like an entrant in some fantastic lunar athletic contest.

Cliff tried to help him with the final adjustments, which were difficult. He did so automatically, because spacemen usually gave each other a hand at that stage. But Breen pushed his hand away.

Obviously, he believed in being independent. Equally obviously, he needed no help.

Being a tyro at that game himself, Cliff reluctantly admired Breen's brisk efficiency. Thanks to it, they were beyond the airlock in only a few minutes and Cliff was leading Breen to the hole through which the *Valier* had fallen.

They approached the brink carefully. Breen reached out and stopped Cliff a few yards from it. He unrolled a length of the ladder and hooked it to his waist-belt. He thrust the rest back at Cliff. Over the radio he said: "Hang on to that tightly. Stay here, and brace yourself. The hole may crumble away near the edge. If I go through, be ready to haul me out."

Again, Cliff had to admire the other's thoroughness. It made sense that Breen should go first, because he was much the lighter. He was less likely to go through the crust; and if he did, he would be the easier to haul out.

Testing the ground at every step, Breen reached the brink without trouble. He had brought with him a hand-lamp considerably more powerful than Cliff's torch, and now he shone it down through the hole.

Cliff heard him hiss between his teeth. Then: "All right, come on, Page. It's safe enough. So are your friends, it seems."

Bewildered, but hopeful because of the last enigmatic remark, Cliff joined Breen and peered down. He almost tumbled into the hole through sheer surprise.

The *Valier* was visible in the inky water below – but only just. It floated largely submerged, like a heavy log. One spacesuited figure stood on the hull, looking up at them, while another was helping a third to emerge from the airlock. Then all three of them were standing up in the lamp's light and waving a greeting. It was impossible to tell which was which.

Breen pointedly tapped his own helmet and equally pointedly touched the radio tuning dial in its little box on his left sleeve. One of the figures got the idea at once (Cliff was sure it was Magnus) and started playing with the dial on its arm.

"Come in, *Valier* . . . Come in, *Valier* . . ." Breen repeated slowly, at intervals.

Soon there was an answer. "Magnus here. All safe here. Is one of you Cliff?"

"Yes," answered Cliff, a lot happier now.

"Well done, old lad. Now, how do we get up there?"

"I'm dropping you a ladder," broke in Breen. "Just wait while I fix the other end." He stared around, picked on a small but solid-looking spur of rock a few yards away, and began to make the ladder fast to it.

Meanwhile, Cliff, who'd taken over the lamp, said: "Look, Magnus, I'm shining the light a bit to your right. Can you see the raft there? Yes? Well, just at the far side of it there's a black hump. Can you make it out?"

"Yes," said Magnus. "What is it?"

"I don't know, but it's artificial and I'm sure it's not something the decapods left."

"I'll take a look at it."

"But how are you going to reach it, Magnus?"

"We'll see."

Breen returned. Naturally, he had heard the conversation on his radio. "Never mind that thing now, Magnus, it'll keep," he said. "I want to get you all out of there."

He pushed the remainder of the ladder over the brink. It fell, unrolling, and the bottom draped across the *Valier*. There seemed to be a short argument down there, carried out by gestures, about who should ascend first; and then one of the trio began climbing.

"Rodney Boland coming up," reported Magnus.

Cliff and Breen helped Rodney over the edge, and then Bill came up. Now it was Magnus's turn, but he seemed to be in no hurry. Carefully, he rolled up and tied the bottom of the ladder so that it swung freely a few inches above the water. Then, clinging to the lower rungs, he began to swing to and fro on it, giving a little kick against the ship each time he passed over it, to gain momentum.

"Enough of that, Magnus," said Breen, sharply. "Come on up."

"Receiving you Strength One, signals indistinct," came Magnus's voice. "Suggest your microphone is faulty."

Breen rounded on Cliff. "Can *you* hear me?"

"What's that, sir?" asked Cliff, blandly, having heard perfectly.

Breen growled. The microphone was a fixture inside the space-helmet, and he couldn't examine it until he was in a position to remove the helmet. So now he could do nothing but beckon Magnus imperiously to come up. It was quite easy for Magnus to avoid noticing this, for the long shallow arc of his swing was carrying him almost to the raft.

Suddenly, nearing the turning point of a swing, he went rapidly hand under hand down to the very end of the ladder, and one reaching foot hooked on to the edge of the raft and dragged it back under him. It was very nicely judged. Instead of swinging back and down into the water, he landed squarely on the raft as it glided beneath him. The impetus carried him and the raft almost back to the *Valier*. He had kept his grip on the ladder, which he now unrolled once more. He tied one end to a loop on the raft, and the comfortable amount of slack drooped into the water.

Then he paddled back to the black hump.

All this time Cliff had been directing the lamp's beam to assist Magnus. Now he became aware of Breen watching him closely through his face-plate. It was dawning upon Breen that they had ganged up against him. Suddenly, he snatched the lamp from Cliff and turned it off. Magnus was left in the dim, practically useless, light of the stars and fungi.

"You can't do that, sir!" said Cliff, sharply.

"Can you tell me why not, Page?" said Breen, very quietly.

"Because that thing down there – whatever it is – is dangerously slippery. Magnus might miss his footing on it in the dark. If he falls in the water, he'll be lost."

"My orders were that he leave it alone. If he would kindly do so, then there's no danger – he has only to climb the ladder."

"But he can't hear your orders, sir."

"That's odd, Page, because obviously you can – now. And yet I'm hardly more than whispering."

Cliff realized that he had been neatly trapped, and was silent. With the puzzled Rodney and Bill lying alongside him, he gazed anxiously down into the gloom. Suddenly, he grinned to himself. All at once a light had come into being down there, and was moving gently. He might have guessed that Magnus would have had the foresight to bring a torch with him when he left the *Valier*.

Breen was stymied and plainly very angry. Metaphorically, steam was coming from the joints of his spacesuit. He got up and stamped around the hole until Cliff was afraid more ground would cave in. It was maddening for Breen. He couldn't abandon Magnus down there. He was forced to await his pleasure. The others didn't know of Breen's interview before leaving Two. It was with Beckworth Bruce, one of this period's great characters and heroes, leader of both the first and second Venus expeditions, and a powerful man at the Scientific Bureau.

Bruce, who was ageing but vigorous in a quiet, steely way, and known popularly as "Baldy" for patent reasons, had sent for Breen and asked: "Is the search tractor ready to leave?"

"Yes, sir."

"Then I want you to take it out personally. On board the

29

Valier, wherever the darned thing is, are a couple of S.I.D. men vitally important to my expedition. They're the only two members who have actually landed on Venus before. I want them brought straight here, without delay. One of them, Martin Magnus, is a troublesome character – ill-disciplined, you know. He's one of Doran's favourites, and in my opinion Doran has allowed him too much rope."

"I see, sir." As Breen well knew, Doran was the chief of the S.I.D., back in London.

"He has an assistant with him, a rather green young boy named Page. But a good lad, none the less. Come to that, Magnus is a good type, too – the star S.I.D. man, in fact. Unfortunately, he's only too aware of it. He needs firm handling. From all accounts, you're the man to do it, and you'd best get in at the start. Put him on a tight rein and ride him that way. I don't want him upsetting things here – planning this expedition is giving me enough headaches. It'll be your job to keep him in his place, which is out of my hair. Got it?"

"I'll not give him an inch, sir."

It was mortifying to Breen to recall that boast now. It was true he hadn't given Magnus an inch – but that worthy had helped himself to yards.

While Breen paced furiously about under the stars, the others watched the light beneath. Soon Magnus said: "I'm going down below for a bit – this looks very interesting."

Almost at once, the light dimmed, then disappeared. Greatly daring, Magnus had worked his way under the mysterious hump, into the body of the thing, below water.

Cliff's nerves crawled with apprehension as he waited.

Hardly a minute later a yelp of alarm came from Magnus. Then the ladder jerked violently and swung. But Magnus's light didn't reappear.

"Sir," called Cliff, urgently, "I think Magnus is in trouble. Bring the lamp."

Breen knew that Baldy Bruce would have no mercy if Magnus were lost through any fault of his. He flung back to the hole and shone the lamp down.

Magnus was climbing the ladder slowly, because he was using only one hand. He was carrying something fairly small in the other, but it wasn't his torch, which he appeared to have lost. When he came within arm's reach, they helped him out. He grinned at Cliff, Bill and Rodney, and ignored Breen.

He said: "I nearly went to the bottom of the drink again.

While I was poking around inside the thing it started to roll. It must have been resting on a submerged rock, and my blundering about disturbed the balance. I only just got out and grabbed the ladder in time. My torch is still down there somewhere."

Breen said, in a voice trembling from his effort to control his anger: "Can you hear my speech now, Magnus?"

"Why, yes, that's a lot better. How on earth did you fix your mike?"

"Would you mind addressing me as 'sir' in future?"

"Darn it," said Magnus. "You've gone again. It must have been a fluke."

"I can hear you, sir," said Cliff, hastily. "I'll relay your messages."

"Thank you, but I'm quite certain there's no need for that," said Breen, coldly. "We shall now proceed at once to the tractor and remove our helmets – together with any doubt about anyone being able to hear anyone."

On the way, Magnus showed Cliff the object he was carrying. It was about a foot square and thin as cardboard, and it was hard even to guess at the material. Although it was patchily stained green and black by the action of the water, which was salty, a pattern of faint lines showed through. There were two small round holes set just inside one edge, as though it were meant to be kept on a file. Cliff could make nothing of it, and gave it back, asking: "What is it?"

"I don't know," said Magnus. "It was the nearest loose object inside that thing – I snatched it up just as we started to go down for the last time. The holes seem to have been drilled, and therefore those lines mightn't be just natural marks, but may mean something. I guess we'll have to clean it up before we're sure."

They passed into the tractor one by one, and settled down, removing their helmets. It was too crowded in there now for them to go the whole hog and get out of their suits. Breen told the driver "Back to Base."

And off they went, bumping gently and swaying towards the sunlight.

"Now," said Breen, "I have no actual authority to put you under arrest, Magnus, but Beckworth Bruce has. And you can bet I'll request him to do so the moment we return. We don't have much trouble at the Base – very little since I've been in charge there. But we do have a punishment cell and, by heaven, before this day is over you'll see the inside of it."

"I'll be delighted to inspect it, if you insist," said Magnus, mildly. He produced a wafer of gum from a clip in his helmet and began to chew. "Oh, I beg your pardon," he said, muffledly, and proffered another wafer to Breen.

Breen turned his back on him. Rodney and Bill exchanged grins with Cliff. Magnus traced the letter on Breen's back with a gentle forefinger. He recited, almost – but not quite – under his breath:

"B is for Big-head, Bumptious and Bold,
Also for Breen, who caught a bad cold."

Breen's ears went redder than his hair, but he affected not to hear. Magnus fell to examining his queer find, and became so preoccupied that Cliff asked Rodney to explain how the *Valier* had come to the surface.

"It was so simple that even Bill here might have thought of it," said Rodney with a smile. "Yet none of us did – except Magnus, and he was slow to arrive at it. Just after you left he was kicking himself all around the cabin, for there was no need for you to have gone. You see, it was only the water in the tank which was keeping us down. Normally, as you know, the tank is filled by an intake pump. All we had to do was reverse that pump and pump the water *out*. Like a submarine, we blew our tanks, so to speak, and up we came. But darned slowly. We were scared we wouldn't quite make it. We only just did."

"Perhaps my being out of it made just the difference," said Cliff.

"Maybe," said Rodney. "Even then we came up with the airlock door still under water, and to get it uppermost Magnus had to give a squirt on the side-jet."

"I missed some fun," said Cliff, "but I had some fun of my own."

He told them of his scramble to the lunar surface. They listened, while Magnus cleaned up the square object with a cloth and some petrol, listening with one ear but looking hard all the time at the marks he was bringing into clearer view.

As Cliff finished his story the three domes of Base Two appeared above the horizon. The tractor ran up to the nearest, and pressed its buffer against the large button on the airlock door. The great door swung slowly open, and the tractor edged through into the lock. The door closed behind it, and air began to fill the big chamber.

Then the further door opened before them, revealing the passage leading down into the Base itself, which lay largely underground.

They were free now to dismount, remove their suits, and make themselves at home – so far as Breen and Baldy Bruce would allow them to.

*

Beckworth Bruce was no taller than Breen, but once he had been. Encroaching age had shrunken him.

"Come, now, Magnus," he said, leaning his elbows on his desk and unconsciously placing his withered hands in an attitude of prayer, "we're responsible adults and we have a big job to do. Let's not act like sulking children. I'm surprised at you."

"No, you're not," contradicted Magnus, flatly.

Bruce ignored that. "All you have to do is tender a perfectly formal apology to the Chief here –"

"Bring on the tumbrils," said Magnus, stonily. "Carry me off to that cell I've heard about – I'm tired."

"This attitude won't get you anywhere," said Bruce, impatiently.

"I'm not trying to get anywhere – except to bed," said Magnus.

"You'll find it a hard bed," Breen informed him, grimly.

"For the last time – will you apologize?" rapped out Bruce.

Magnus said: "What the dickens have I to apologize for? Cliff and I made a discovery which I think is of first-rate importance, even if you don't. There is, or has been, another intelligent race on the Moon that nobody dreamed existed, that even the decapods, who lived here, knew nothing of. How could I leave a thing like that and hurry home to tea just because teacher here bawled at me? I bring you concrete evidence." He pointed to the square plate which lay on Bruce's desk beside the little meter Cliff had found. "And you don't even consider it. You waste everyone's time playing this idiotic game of soldiers – and you accuse *me* of being childish!"

"Breen was acting under my orders –"

"So I've gathered," cut in Magnus.

"The point is this: the second Venus expedition, under my command, *is* like a military operation. If it's to succeed, then people can't go riding off on their pet hobby-horses just when they fancy. There must be discipline. I want you to understand that now. Archæology is all very well in its place. But we're concerned immediately with our own living race, not an alien dead one. We've got to establish habitable areas on Venus and other planets. If not, then our own race may become only of archæological interest. You're supposed to be blazing the trail for us,

33

not chasing after every red herring that crops up. You see, I know you of old, Magnus. Every time you get your teeth into something a bit odd, you won't – or can't – let go until you've dug down to the root of it."

"I don't dig with my teeth," Magnus objected.

"That characteristic is admirable in ordinary circumstances," continued Bruce. "But these are not ordinary circumstances. We're racing against time. Can't you get that into your head?"

"All right, Baldy, you have a point," admitted Magnus. "But just answer me one question. In beginning a big military operation, is it wise to risk having your Base overrun by an enemy you aren't even aware of?"

"What do you mean?"

"Do I have to remind you that in the rosy days of old Smith this same Base was so overrun – by the decapods? Regarding archæology – I don't know about that plate, but I'll warrant you that little meter isn't so very old. That submarine was in service within your lifetime, I'll gamble – perhaps even since we've been on the Moon."

"Submarine?" Both Bruce and Breen echoed the word together.

"Yes. I had only a few seconds to look around before the thing sank. The water had rotted a lot of stuff in there – it was a mess. But it stuck out a mile that it was a midget submarine – or rather, half of one – which had run aground on a submerged rock and broken its back. Probably the other half is on the bottom somewhere there, too – maybe it contains the bodies of the crew. Or body, shall we say, for it was so small it looked more like a one-man effort. Of course, it mightn't have been even that. Perhaps there wasn't any crew. It could have been a robot submarine, sent out scouting, just as we sent small scout rockets ahead of us to Venus. How do we know it wasn't scouting to find – *us*?"

Bruce picked up the two objects and examined them closely.

Suddenly, he said: "I'm reporting this to Doran right away. You stand by, Magnus – he'll probably want to question you."

"Aren't I going to see my bed tonight?" grumbled Magnus.

Bruce pulled the Visi a little nearer and got on to the operator.

"Put me through to Mr. Doran."

"Yes, sir," said the operator's bright image, and then the screen went blank. A couple of minutes later, the calm and distinguished features of Doran appeared. He still affected to part his white hair on the wrong side, and there was a carnation in his button-hole. He looked as fresh and easy as if he were just off to his club, but he had been sitting in that office in the tall white building in Trafalgar Square all day handling crises and problems from all corners of man's empire above and below the sea, on Earth or far away from Earth. The picture of him danced a bit and occasionally showers of white spots fled across it, for on the Earth-Moon TV link there was always interference from the sun's hard radiations.

"Hello, Baldy, what is it now? *Archimedes the Second* giving trouble again?"

"No, Doran, she's fine – passed all her final tests. I see no reason why we shouldn't start in a week's time, on the dot. It's something new now – your curly-headed boy, Magnus, has arrived."

"It's funny," said Doran, jovially, "but everywhere he goes he trails trouble as though it were mud on his boots. Hello, there, Magnus – in your element?"

"Oh, quite," said Magnus, sarcastically. "I'm in jail – almost."

"What's that?"

It took quite a lot of explaining. So did Magnus's theories.

"I see," said Doran, at length. "Nice work, Magnus. I feel it should be rewarded. How about a week in that condemned cell, as Baldy suggests?"

Magnus scowled, and Breen looked hopeful. Bruce smiled a tight smile.

"You must realize, Magnus, that I can't undermine Bruce's authority," went on Doran. "Besides, I've thought for a long time that your comb needs cutting. Manners makyth man, you know. I'm sure one week's solitary confinement, on bread and water, will calm that evil temper of yours. Sentence confirmed, Baldy."

Breen smiled for the first time that day. Magnus's scowl deepened.

Doran said: "Let me have another look at that thing Magnus found."

"Surely," said Bruce, and held it close to the Visi screen.

"Confound this interference!" exclaimed Doran, presently. "I can't see it very clearly, but I'll tell you what it looks like to me: a map of a lunar crater, with precious few surrounding features."

"Right on the nose, Doran," said Magnus, sardonically. "It must be your lucky day."

Doran looked pleased, then concentrated on the plate again.

Finally, he shook his head. "I give up. I can't identify it. Can you, Baldy?"

Bruce pored over it, but couldn't get a clue.

"You try, Breen," Doran suggested.

But Breen, after a couple of guesses which further study made him withdraw, was no help, and became angry with himself for falling down on a job.

"All right, Magnus," said Doran, irritable now. "Where is it?"

"I don't know," said Magnus, looking faintly amused at the flushed Breen.

Doran studied Magnus's expression.

"But you've got a pretty strong suspicion, haven't you?" he said, shrewdly.

"I have an opinion, certainly."

"Well, let's hear it."

"No," said Magnus. "I'll mull it over in the seclusion of my little cell. I'll have plenty of time, thanks to you. Of course, if you choose to revoke the sentence . . ."

"Sorry, nothing doing – I'm not bargaining," said Doran. "Show Magnus to his room, Breen."

Magnus stamped out like a petulant boy, with Breen close at his heels.

"He'll cool off," said Doran. "Show Cross that plate over the Visi. Wire him a photo if he can't see enough detail – you'd better have it cleaned up some more first. Cross will identify it, if anyone can. Anything else?"

"Not at the moment, old man. I'm arranging for the *Valier* to be salvaged, and a search made for this submarine thing – both halves."

"Good. Then I'll leave that to you." Doran's image faded.

Cross was the old astronomer at Base One. One was hewn and tunnelled out of a great cliff, the Straight Wall, lying some two hundred miles from Two. On top of the Wall was an astronomical observatory where Cross now lived every minute of his dedicated life, using a large magnification on his telescope in this almost airless world, mapping the farthest reaches of the universe.

Bruce got in touch with him at once. The old man studied the plate through the Visi and grumbled: "It could be any one of a score of craters. Depends how big it is. Isn't there a scale on the confounded thing?"

"Not that I'm aware of."

"Then it's necessary to examine the surrounding detail more closely. Wire me a copy."

"All right," said the disappointed Bruce. "And I'll have it cleaned up for you."

After Cross had received the photograph sent electrically through the cable linking the Bases, nothing was heard from him for more than five hours. Then he rang up and told Bruce: "I haven't got anywhere and I don't look like getting anywhere. The two curved ridges, one north and one south of the crater, look to me like the horns of a ruined ring. But, confound it, I've compared it with every similar known feature on the Moon, and it doesn't fit. So I can make only three guesses. Either it's a crater on the back of the Moon in an area we haven't completely mapped yet. Or it's a purely imaginative drawing. Or it's a portrait of the artist, who presumably is or was an oyster."

Bruce sighed. "All right, Cross, if you can't dream up something better than that you'd best go to bed."

Cross mumbled something about "Base ingratitude," which might or might not have been a pun, and disappeared. Bruce sighed again, got Doran on the Visi, and submitted his negative report.

Doran said: "If Cross doesn't know, then I doubt if the Astronomer Royal will. Anyhow, we can't see it properly from here . . ." He looked resigned, and said: "In every official's life there comes a time when, loathing himself, he has to cry: 'Send for Magnus!' So – do so, Baldy."

When, in his own good time, Magnus came shambling in, Doran said: "Magnus, you're reprieved. Congratulations. Now, where the devil is this crater – in your opinion?"

"In the Mare Serenitatis."

"Nonsense!" Doran exclaimed. "If it were, Cross would never have missed it."

"It's Linné," said Magnus.

"Linné? You mean, *before* . . .?"

Magnus nodded. "I think so. I've always been very interested in the Linné affair, and I remember the old maps I studied. I've tried once or twice to get these Base johnnies to organize an expedition to it, but they think like Baldy here – noses are meant to be applied to grindstones and not poked into queer corners for the sake of it."

They all knew, roughly, the story of Linné, which was an old one but had never properly been investigated.

The most conspicuous crater on the vast flat spread of the Mare Serenitatis was Bessel, twelve miles across. In the eighteen-forties and fifties Linné was listed as the second most conspicuous crater on the Mare, being six miles across and about a thousand feet deep. It was measured, and drawn on maps, many times. Yet in 1866 a German astronomer, Schmidt, was examining the Mare through his telescope when suddenly he became aware that Linné had vanished!

All that could be seen in its place was a small white patch. Immediately, there was a world-wide sensation. Hundreds of telescopes were directed at the mysterious white patch, and later it became clear that actually it was a low dome with a very small central hole in the apex.

Some theories held that it was the result of a moonquake. Others, that a large meteorite had obliterated the crater. But none was wholly satisfying, and Linné was still a mystery.

"If it is so," said Doran, slowly, "it dates your map to sometime before eighteen sixty-six. So your submarine isn't so recent, after all."

"By that argument the British Museum dates back to twelve hundred and fifteen because it contains Magna Carta," said Magnus, sarcastically. "In my opinion, the submarine isn't more than fifty years old, maybe only twenty – maybe only one. Perhaps Cliff Page has some ideas on it – he's the only other person who saw it. He's a marine biologist and probably knows more about sea corrosion than I do."

They sent for Cliff but, as he pointed out, he had seen only the outer surface of the craft and therefore could hazard no guess, not knowing of what substance it was composed. If it were very old, he personally would have expected to find it encrusted with more deposit than it was.

Doran digested this, and then said: "I've been checking up with our old friend, the leader of the decapods. He knew nothing of any cavern in the area where the *Valier* landed, so evidently it doesn't join at any point with their particular underground sea. He knew even less of the submarine, which bewilders him. So that's that – we begin from scratch."

"We begin from Linné, if you ask me," said Magnus.

"That'll have to be left to Breen," said Bruce. "*Archimedes Two* takes off only a week from now and I want you and Page to be aboard it."

Magnus said: "A couple of men with a relief driver could get there in three days – it will still be daylight all along the route for the next week, so they could drive round the clock. Say they spend a whole day investigating Linné. Then, with luck, they may take only two days on the return trip, for they'll have

38

blazed the trail. That totals only six days, leaving a full day for rest before the take-off ... Would you care to come with me, Cliff?"

Cliff nodded eagerly, and Bruce broke out into a querulous piping of protest.

"Suppose you get lost? Or the tractor breaks down? Or you run into whoever sent that submarine – and they aren't friendly? I won't have the expedition jeopardized by foolhardy young – "

"Baldy, you must be getting old," Doran broke in. "Remember, you were young and foolhardy once. If you hadn't been, someone other than Beckworth Bruce would have been the first man to land on Mars. Apart from that, if intelligent but unknown beings have been roaming near Base Two, as it seems they have, I want to know all about it – and smartly, too. This Linné business must be cleared up sooner or later, anyhow. Magnus is the right man for the job and he's on the spot and his timetable sounds feasible."

Bruce threw up his hands. "You're the Director."

"That's right," said Doran. "By the way, young Page, there's another thing I want cleared up. Brcen has reported to me that you were responsible for the loss of the *Valier*."

"That's true, sir," said Cliff, his enthusiasm meeting sudden death.

"Rubbish!" snorted Magnus. "The *Valier* isn't lost – she can be salvaged. It was merely bad luck that Cliff happened to put her down on a thin spot in the crust – nobody could have known it was there. He made a perfect landing."

"Maybe he did – but in the wrong place: outside the perimeter," said Doran. "Watch that in future, Page."

"Yes, sir."

The screen went blank, and Cliff realized with relief that he had got off extremely lightly.

CHAPTER THREE

INSIDE LINNÉ

Doran had judged Magnus's timetable feasible. Both men were over-optimistic.

The way had been long, devious and tough. The tractor had ground along north-west to the Sinus Æstuum and then, to avoid the towering range of the lunar Apennines, swung on to the smooth Mare Vaporum and proceeded along its northern boundary to the worst section of the trip, the Hæmus Mountains. Some of the peaks here rose to 8,000 feet, and the valleys between them wound like snakes.

Here it was that the timetable went wrong and the travellers lost the best part of a day. Too many of the valleys, which on the map appeared to be open-throated, turned out to be blind at the far end. And too often it was a very far end, and retracing their tracks was a weary business, enlivened only by the colourful curses Magnus brought down on the heads of all selenographers.

But Mac, the regular driver, was a good one; and from the way Magnus handled a lunar tractor one might have thought it was a London taxi. Cliff, of course, was the novice again, and did most of his stretch over the easy "Sea of Vapours." But by the end of it he had become a really competent driver. He was glad of this opportunity to learn, for fully-fledged S.I.D. men had to be jacks of all trades and be able to pilot everything between and including submarines and spaceships.

Mac, a quiet individual, rather homesick – when off-duty he was often gazing longingly at Earth, which hung perpetually up there against the back-cloth of stars – juggled the tractor through the last pass. And so at last they had broken out on to the Mare Serenitatis and it was a straight run, almost due north, to the flawed remains of the small walled plain at the edge of which Linné stood.

Mac was able to step the speed up to forty miles an hour now, but so smooth was the going that Cliff was able to make and pour tea and hand it round. It was very cosy inside the tractor. Yet only a couple of inches' thickness of slightly darkened and treated plastic hood stood between them and the naked heat of the sun which would have boiled their blood to vapour, the ultra-violet rays which would have blinded them, and the near-vacuum which would have suffocated them.

So the voyagers, in their little land cockleshell, cheating many kinds of death, rode gaily across the vast, baking, glaring Mare – sipping tea.

At length the uneven ridge of the broken, semi-circular wall began to show above the slightly convex horizon, and they began a detour eastwards to skirt the end of it.

And then – Linné.

Magnus and Cliff couldn't take their eyes off it as they approached, and even Mac forgot about Earth for a while. Certainly Linné had shrunk. There are many thousands of lunar mounds, some only twenty feet high, while others are sizeable hills. This was a sizeable hill, but nothing like the size of the crater Linné had once been. Moreover, the curve of its dome-like shape was surprisingly flat. It was strikingly lighter in colour than the surrounding plain.

Mac stopped the tractor at the foot of it and waited for orders.

Magnus and Cliff surveyed the white swelling lump ahead of them.

"I think the tractor will be able to get up it, don't you?" said Cliff.

"Sure," said Magnus. "Easily – I doubt if we'll have to go below second gear. Straight up, Mac."

The tractor began climbing. Again Magnus had been over-optimistic. They soon found bottom gear was a necessity, for the slope was unusually smooth and the caterpillar tracks sometimes lost their grip and the tractor slid and slewed about.

"I've never met anything like this before," said Magnus, frowning.

They ground uncertainly onwards and up. Nothing new came into sight: the dome was featureless to all appearances. It was as though they were crawling over the top of a giant white billiard ball.

Then the gradient eased, beginning to level off.

"We're near the centre," said Magnus. "Keep your eyes skinned, Mac. There's a deep crater there somewhere and we don't want to take a header into it."

"It's right in front," said Cliff. "About a couple of hundred yards off."

"Stop her," said Magnus, and Mac braked. "We'll walk the rest. You stay here, Mac, and we'll keep in touch with you by radio."

He and Cliff struggled into their spacesuits, tuned in the radio sets, collected a camera and a brace of powerful hand-lamps, and stepped out through the airlock.

There was a fine all-round view of the plain, with the dome curving, blindingly white, in all directions down towards it.

"Gosh, now I know how a fly feels on Baldy's pate," said Magnus.

Cliff laughed, but he was eager to look into the crater, took a pace towards it, and his leaden soles skidded on the smooth surface.

"Careful," warned Magnus.

"What *is* this stuff?" asked Cliff, stamping a foot on it.

"I've no idea. It looks like marble, but I don't see how it could be."

They shelved that query, and walked on towards the crater.

Only, it wasn't a crater, after all – not a natural one, anyway. To begin with, it was perfectly circular and about a hundred yards in diameter. The sun was almost directly overhead and striking right down into it, showing the pair that they were standing dizzily on the lip of a deep cylindrical hole. But what caught the eye at once was the spiral of a wide groove winding its way at gentle slope around and down the interior walls, down into the black pool of darkness lying below the farthest reaches of the sun's rays.

Magnus and Cliff looked at that and then at each other.

Magnus's voice echoed in Cliff's helmet: "Artificial! The whole darned heap is artificial. I'd suspected it on the way up."

"Whoever could have built such a tremendous thing?"

"That's what we're here to find out," said Magnus. "I wish we had more time. We'll have to start back in a few hours or we'll miss the boat and there'll be the devil to pay. Someone else will have the fun of exploring this ant heap. Oh, well, it's been here long enough – since the eighteen-sixties, obviously. We've established one basic fact: whatever happened to Linné wasn't an accident of nature. Look at that groove."

They both did so, again.

It was an odd formation. Ten feet below where they stood a six-foot wide flat shelf ran around the shaft. It curved widely away on either side of them, to join itself a hundred yards away on the far side of the gulf. But there was one gap in it, and that was where the spiral groove, which was of the same width, began.

If one jumped that gap each time (it was about ten feet across: an easy jump on the Moon) one could circle the shelf forever. If instead one chose the downward path beginning there, it would lead one down the spiral, passing under itself continuously, down into the unknown.

Magnus took a couple of photographs.

"D'you know what it reminds me of?" he asked, suddenly, and supplied the answer: "The rifling inside the barrel of a piece of artillery."

Cliff, too, had seen big guns in museums, and nodded, but without enthusiasm. He said, dubiously: "Supposing this is an enormous gun, meant for firing outsize shells at Earth?"

"If it is," said Magnus, half seriously, "it's been here for a long time without being used, so far as we know. Look, I know we really haven't much time, but how about going down for a look-see? We can't very well pass up this chance."

"No, I suppose not," said Cliff. "I hope, though, that on the way down we don't meet a shell on the way up."

He wasn't so much bothered by that possibility as by the one of slipping on this treacherously smooth stuff and falling right out of the comparatively narrow groove. For the sides of this great hole were sheer, and heights – or depths – worried him and unsettled his stomach.

Magnus radioed Mac to put him in the picture and warn him that if they went very deep then it was unlikely they'd be able to reach him again by radio.

"Supposing you don't come up?" asked Mac.

Magnus considered. "We'll be up again within two hours," he promised.

"I hope so," said Mac. "We're well behind schedule and I'm not too sure of finding the way back through that devil's maze in the Hæmus range."

"I'll find it," said Magnus, airily. "Come on, Cliff."

He leaped lightly down on to the flat shelf. To Cliff it presented itself as merely a ribbon edging an abyss, and he groaned. Then he lowered himself gingerly from the top rim, hanging by his hands and keeping his face close to the wall. Then he dropped the remaining yard or so.

They began the long winding journey down, and Cliff continued to hug the wall.

They'd circled the shaft only twice and descended only thirty feet when Magnus, who was leading, stopped suddenly. He pointed just ahead at the path. Neatly in its centre a pair of parallel grooves began, a yard apart.

"Grooves within grooves," said Magnus.

43

"They look like train lines," said Cliff.

The "train lines" continued to run down ahead of them as they went deeper and deeper, speculating. After half an hour they reached the frontier of shadow. Above, the grooved sunlit walls seemed to converge and form a shining, inverted funnel. Below, intense blackness lay like a solid thing. The beams of their lamps cut into it, and from what little they illuminated the pattern appeared to continue as before.

They had trouble in hearing Mac on the radio now, but they managed to get through to him a report on their present position. Then they went on, down into the darkness.

Cliff had already slipped several times. That had scared him enough in the daylight. But the thought of it happening in the dark made him tread very warily indeed.

His imagination began to get out of hand. He pictured strange eyes in strange faces watching from below, watching their lamps as they swung along and down. Or even, perhaps, watching their faces, watching with eyes for which this darkness was light.

But that was rubbish, he told himself, not very convincingly.

Beings of some sort had built this place, carved or moulded the groove-path he was treading. Likely they built that submarine too. And that wasn't so old.

It must have taken a lot of them to do all this. Surely they couldn't have all died suddenly. They must still be around – somewhere.

It was comforting to recall they were intelligent. On Earth, intelligence usually went hand in hand with civilization, and civilization argued some moral sense. They wouldn't attack harmless strangers. Or would they? Men were supposed to have been civilized for centuries, and yet only recently had grown out of murderous wars and persecution even unto death of those who thought differently from them.

Magnus stopped so suddenly that Cliff ran into him and, being over-tense, gave a little cry of alarm.

"It's all right, Cliff," said Magnus. "I'm only trying to walk through a wall."

He examined it by the light of his lamp.

"No, a door," he amended.

There was certainly the outline of something that looked like a shut door, though neither hinges nor handle was discernible. It was almost as wide as the path and some eight feet tall.

Magnus stepped aside to let Cliff see it. Cliff took a pace forward and then from the corner of his face-plate glimpsed something which shot cold fear through him.

Magnus had stepped too far and slipped over the edge of the groove-path. He fell into darkness and his lamp went whirling away – and then, it seemed, the lamp was caught and held by an invisible hand. It hung there, apparently in space, shining like a beacon.

As Cliff stood petrified, Magnus's voice sounded: "Confound it – I'll break my neck yet!"

Cliff came to life again, and flashed his lamp in that general direction. "Magnus, where are you?"

His lamp answered the question silently, its beam alighting on Magnus, who lay spread-eagled on his back only a yard below the edge of the groove and a few feet from his lamp, which, like he, rested on the level bottom of the shaft.

Cliff laughed through sheer relief and went and helped Magnus to his feet. Then together they made the circuit of the bottom, of whose proximity they hadn't been aware. So far as they could see, apart from themselves it was as bare as an empty dinner plate. They came back to the door at the groove's end because there was no other feature of interest.

"There must be a way of opening it," said Magnus. "Ah! What's this?"

"This" was a small black button set in the wall just beside the door.

"I wonder if anyone's at home?" said Magnus, and pressed the button before Cliff had time to consider the consequences.

The consequences were several and prompt. It was as though the darkness were blown to nothingness by an exploding bomb of light. The white walls, the grooves, and the floor itself all gleamed with light.

The door at the end of the groove sailed upwards and disappeared in the thickness of the wall above. A similar door, but very much bigger, whose existence they had not detected, performed the same trick at the far side of the shaft. In both cases a large, bright-lit and perfectly empty room was revealed beyond.

"No," said Magnus, in a moment. "There's no one at home."

Cliff wasn't so sure. He looked around uneasily and peered up the shaft.

"Look, Magnus," he said, a little hoarsely, and pointed up. Magnus looked. The shaft, which had been two-thirds sunlit and one-third in shadow, was now lit up every foot of its height – but not by sunlight. The light seemed to come from the walls themselves. Quite clearly it showed the top of the shaft, no longer a small hole with a view of an incongruous black sky and bright sun, but a neat, gleaming disc, looking from this distance like a silver coin.

"H'm," was Magnus's comment. "It's nice to have a roof over our heads. At least, it'll keep the rain out."

Cliff grunted. "Yes – and keep us in."

"We'll worry about that later," said Magnus. "Let's see what we've got here."

He started towards the smaller room. Cliff caught his arm. "I know what you're going to say," said Magnus, instantly. "It may be a trap."

"It may be a trap," said Cliff before he could stop himself.

They laughed.

"There's only one way to find out," said Magnus. "You wait outside."

He walked through the doorway.

"Windows!" he said, in surprise. And then, a few moments later, in even greater surprise: "Good heavens!"

"What is it?" Cliff asked, uneasily.

In a minute, Magnus said: "Come and take a look at this."

Still cautious, Cliff edged through, ready to leap back if the door showed any sign of coming down. But it didn't.

It was a long and narrow room. The farther wall was blank, but both side walls bore small windows. Magnus was standing at one of them, and Cliff joined him.

He found he was looking down on a vast floor-space which was quite a hundred feet below. It was lit by the same mysterious agency as the shaft. Several huge machines of different designs stood around, a couple of them all of sixty feet tall and long in proportion. Some of them looked like lathes, some like dynamos, some looked like nothing on Earth. None of them appeared to be working. Nor did anything living move among them.

"Workshop," said Magnus, briefly. "Now take a peep through the other window at the living quarters."

Cliff crossed to the other side of the room.

In a moment he said "Good heavens!" also.

Down below, in orderly arrangement on the floor, were tables, chairs, stools and benches, of simple design, much like mediæval furniture on Earth. But there were two striking differences. All these objects were fashioned from the now familiar white stone. And they could only have been so fashioned for giants.

"Well," said Magnus, "we've learned something more. Whoever dwelt here had – or have – some things in common with us. They need light to see by and chairs to sit on. And I'd say this was a lunar Base, the same in principle as ours: obviously it's airtight, for the doors and the roof of the shaft out there form a great airlock. Therefore they breathe as we do – though it may be a different kind of atmosphere. There's just one little thing that scares me: the scale of that furniture. The tops of those tables are twenty feet from the floor. The people who used 'em must be around twice that height – say, forty feet tall!"

"Fee, fie, fo, fum . . ." said Cliff, feebly.

Magnus pressed his face-plate against the window, trying to make out something hard to see from this angle.

"Confusion worse confounded!" he muttered. "What do you make of those things leaning against that table – the fourth from the right?"

Cliff peered at them for a long time. "Perhaps I'm mad," he said, "but I can see a darn great sabre about twenty feet long!"

"What else?"

"Well, there's an even longer pitchfork, though it might be a sort of two-pronged spear; and a spiked club that could flatten an elephant; and . . . is that a bow?"

"A bow, I think, and some arrows. And that pyramidal thing might be a helmet – a helmet for Cyclops! This is just crazy – something from a fairy story. Why should people who are obviously very advanced scientifically – ahead of us in some ways, I'd say – arm themselves with crude weapons like those?"

"It could be they went in for amateur theatricals," ventured Cliff, half believing it.

"I've run into some puzzles in my time," said Magnus. "But this . . . Where does the submarine fit into the pattern, I wonder? Anyhow, we know now it couldn't have been manned. One of these giants could scarcely get his legs alone into it. It was a robot sub."

He stubbed his toes in one of the "train lines."

"Another puzzle. These run straight in here from the path at the wall. Why?"

"Because they can't run through the wall," said Cliff, sensibly.

Magnus ignored it. "You know," he said, "I think a sort of train *did* run up and down these lines, and a few trucks at a time were detached and fed into this room. I believe this room is an elevator to take 'em down to that lower floor."

"But they must have been far too small for giants to ride in," objected Cliff.

47

"That's right." Magnus mused, then said: "So they must have carried goods only – supplies for the Base. And where did the supplies come from? The more I think about it, the more I'm sure the shaft out there was built to accommodate spaceships – only one at a time, of course, on the giant scale. The spiral groove winding around it with its little train is a quick method of unloading – more efficient than clumsy cranes and hoists. But they must have been very different spaceships from ours. Imagine trying to land one of our ships in that shaft! And, remember, theirs must be much bigger. They must have complete control of them. And they can't be rockets – you can't land a rocket in a shaft you're pumping full of exhaust gas."

"If their spaceship isn't a rocket, then it must be based on some principle we don't know."

"Exactly," said Magnus. "What does it remind you of?"

"The ship the Venusian came to Earth in – and returned in. That also had no visible jet or means of propulsion. Nobody ever did figure out just how it might have worked. Why, Magnus, do you think a Venusian ship used this place?"

"I think a ship, or ships, of that *kind* did. And maybe still do, for all we know – who's to see them during the long nights? But the Venusians, remember, are subaqueous creatures and can't live out of water. I don't see any aquariums around here. I see only evidences of outsize beings who live and breathe in an atmosphere and seem only too human in some ways. There's nothing at all to connect them with Venus. Another thing puzzles me: the giants couldn't have ridden on the train into here, and so how did they get in and out of the place?"

"No mystery about that," said Cliff. "They just walked through that door on the other side of the shaft. It's nearly fifty feet high, you know. Probably it's another elevator – a passenger lift."

"People tell me my nose is too long. Perhaps they're right. There are times when I can't see beyond it. . . . I wonder how the lifts work?"

Magnus began looking around for anything resembling controls.

"We've no time for that – Mac's waiting," said Cliff, anxiously.

"The cupboard's bare – not a knob or a button anywhere," grumbled Magnus. "Perhaps you have to say 'Open Sesame' aloud or something."

He took some photographs through the windows and said: "Let's look at the other lift."

It turned out to be even more bare, for there weren't any windows. It was like a huge cubical box, fifty feet along every edge. There being nothing to see, they soon emerged. Magnus touched the gleaming wall of the shaft gingerly with his steel gloves.

"My guess," he said, "is that the entire interior surface of this place is coated with some substance that glows brightly when an electric current is passed through it. It must be pretty weak and diffused: I can't feel anything like a shock. I wish we had something like it in our own Bases. We'll have to learn the secret of it, Cliff – it would be a boon to industry on Earth. Maybe some other time. . . . We'd better start back now – it's not going to be easy climbing *up* that darned spiral. Anyhow, we've reached something of a dead end here."

"There's a dead end at the top of the shaft too – now," said Cliff. "How are we going to get out?"

"I don't know. Let's experiment."

Magnus walked back to the smaller door and jabbed at the black button beside it. The light all about them faded right out, but not before they had glimpsed both doors coming down like shutters. Darkness again enfolded them. Cliff looked up and saw that the sun and the stars were once more apparent at the distant top of the shaft.

"H'm," came from Magnus. "Our oversized friends seem to favour all-purpose buttons. And aren't they stingy with them! I bet if I press that same little button again, the light will come on, the doors open, and so forth, just as before."

"Don't – in case something gets stuck," Cliff advised, switching on his lamp. "Let's go: Mac will be having kittens if we don't show up soon."

"All right," said Magnus, reluctantly.

It was an exhausting climb, for although the slope was gradual they kept slipping back one pace out of every three or four.

"I reckon to get around on floors . . . of this stuff . . . those big chaps must have . . . rubber feet," panted Magnus as they emerged into the sun's rays again. He stopped, partly to recover his breath, partly to radio and reassure Mac, who sounded as if he needed reassuring. He told Mac also of their discoveries, but the tractor driver was incurious. He'd been on the Moon too long and was interested in little but getting off it.

They resumed plodding upwards, and at last gained the flat shelf. They paused there, seeking a clue about where the roof had come from. They found one, only because they were looking intently for it: they hadn't noticed it on the way down. It was just a faint line circling the shaft about a foot above the line where the flat shelf joined the wall.

"That section, about a foot thick, must slide right out, like the lid of a pencil box, and cover the whole top," said Magnus. "My young friend, there's a sizeable power plant down below, somewhere. I hope we can come back before the vandals get in and strip the place."

"And I hope we'll come up by train *that* time," said Cliff.

They gained the rim ten feet above by Cliff mounting upon Magnus's shoulders, pulling himself up, then reaching down to give Magnus a hand. Such acrobatics were fairly easy under this weak gravity.

They were on the summit of the dome again and nothing had changed. The tractor and a worried Mac were waiting.

"Two hours?" Mac greeted them. "Over three, by my watch."

"Ah, you forgot to set it back an hour when we crossed the equator," said Magnus, knowingly.

Which was nonsense, but it served to keep Mac quiet and thoughtful until the real problem of the Hæmus Mountains had to be faced again. And then Magnus became really helpful, choosing the quickest route without fail. The result was that they arrived back at Base Two twelve hours later than they should have done – but still twelve hours before *Archimedes II* was due to take off.

Beckworth Bruce's wrath was mitigated by his curiosity about Linné. He was desperately busy with last-minute preparations but he took time off to join in the conference between Doran (on the Visi), Magnus, Cliff and Breen. The Commandant of Base One was also in on it, though only through a sound link.

Everyone examined Magnus's photographs, directly or indirectly, listened to his story, and considered his and Cliff's theories.

Doran was concerned about this evidence of an unknown but plainly formidable race being on the Moon, where man's foothold was not all that secure.

He said: "For centuries the astronomers told us our satellite was a dead world, but we're finding it's quite a box of tricks. First the decapods, and now this . . . this lunar Brobdingnag. Magnus assumes it's a Base, like one of ours, built by and for people – let's call them 'people,' even if they're Titans – visiting the Moon from another planet. I'm not so sure. The Moon once had considerably more atmosphere than it has now, as we know from the decapods. The decapods were driven underground because of the thinning atmosphere. Why not another lunar race also – these Titans? I think the Titans may be living now deep underground, in the Moon's interior, in pressurized caverns. And Linné is their bolt-hole into space, as it were – which they constructed sometime around eighteen-sixty."

"But surely the decapods would have known of them in the ancient days?" said Bruce.

"The decapods!" Doran was always a little scornful of that intelligent but unpractical race. "They live in a daydream – always have done. Why, they didn't even know *we* existed until we broke in on them! The Titans could have lived around the other side of the Moon from them without them ever being aware of it."

The Commandant of Base One said: "We'll have to break in on the Titans also – through Linné. With your permission, sir, I should like to lead a well-armed expedition there."

"Arm your men with stones and slings – most effective against giants, so I've heard," said Magnus, mischievously.

Breen said, primly: "I think that should be a job for our Base, sir. Our driver, Mackay, knows the way – "

"Do you think I can't read maps, Breen?" interrupted the Base One Commandant, coldly.

"Peace, gentlemen," said Doran. "We can't allow either Base to become dangerously undermanned. You will each organize a moderate-sized party – I suggest it be of twenty men – and they will rendezvous at Linné. If you encounter aggressive Titans who attempt to club or spear you, then you'll be at liberty to use your – um – slings. But don't start anything. They might, after all, be friendly, and if so we may learn a lot from them. Well, Baldy, you'd better get back to work. As for you bright brace of Investigators – off to bed for a few hours. I wish you all a calm sea and a prosperous voyage. I'll keep in touch with you all the way. 'Bye for now. And now, Commandant, and you, Breen, regarding your respective expeditions . . ."

It was widely supposed in the Special Investigation Department that Doran slept only every third night, and even then, in his sleep, watched over the fortunes of his men pursuing dangerous missions in the near and far reaches of the solar system.

He had an aptitude for coining fitting name-tags, and following that conference the mysterious giants of Linné were always referred to as "the Titans." And Magnus and Cliff referred to

51

them often that night in their bunks for, tired as they were, they did not find it easy to drift off to sleep. For they were turning their backs on one mystery only to voyage to a planet that was still ninety-nine per cent mystery.

CHAPTER FOUR

VENUS REVISITED

The first *Archimedes* had been a big ship. Her successor was far bigger, and from her exterior size one might have judged even a family of Titans would have found her roomy.

Actually, she was nine-tenths nothing but a water tank.

She had been designed and built at record speed. Indeed, the draughtsmen were shaping her with quick, chisel-edged pencils within hours of the original *Archimedes* beginning the return journey from the planet on which she had failed to land.

Archimedes could have landed on Venus, but only at the cost of using up her last few tons of water propellant. She had been built in the hope that there was water on the planet and she could refill her tanks there to take off again for Earth. And in fact there was water on Venus, but only, so far as had been discovered, in the form of one small lake.

Therein dwelt the Venusians, large jellyfish of an indeterminate kind, quite transparent under water except for a single tiny eye. And as they had never been out of water (and almost certainly couldn't live or move out of that element) they had never really been seen at all.

But they had been felt.

They had enormous strength and a respectable technical ability, for somehow or other (the way was still a mystery) they had built at least one spaceship, in which one of their kind had voyaged to Earth, kidnapped Cliff's brother, Kenneth, and taken him back to Venus. Magnus and Cliff had followed in *Archimedes*, with Beckworth Bruce in charge.

Playing safe, Bruce put *Archimedes* in an orbit about Venus and sent Magnus and Cliff down in a small scout-rocket to reconnoitre the lake and report whether it would be all right for the larger ship to land. They rescued Kenneth Page, but barely escaped with their lives from the Venusians, who started a gas attack from the lake.

So *Archimedes* had to return with only part of its mission fulfilled. And of all Venus only a limited area around the lake had been explored. However, Magnus and Cliff found breathable air there, and also plant-bearing soil. And although there was a perpetual mist because the clouds reached everywhere to the ground, and the light was dull and the aspect gloomy, there seemed good chances of a human colony being able to settle there – provided a reasonable water supply was obtainable. In case it was not, *Archimedes II* carried enough water to make a round trip.

Previously, Venus had been surveyed by robot scout-rockets which sent radar pulses down through the all-enveloping clouds and recorded a rough map of the terrain. In some places the map showed moderately regular formations, which might possibly be towns of some kind – and just as possibly mere freak markings of nature.

It was planned to land *Archimedes II* near one of the smallest of these formations, some fifty miles from the dangerous lake. The idea was that if such areas were habitations of intelligent beings who turned out to be as unfriendly as the other kind of Venusians, then a small community of them would be easier to deal with than a large one.

Archimedes II had been built on the Moon, near Base Two, from metal mined from that mineral-rich locality, and filled to the capacity of its tanks with water pumped from the underground sea where formerly the decapods lived.

The take-off of the largest spaceship ever built by man was a real event, and all the world watched it on their TV sets. (The cameras were on cables run out from Base Two.)

It was far easier than such a take-off would have been from Earth, for a speed of only two miles per second was necessary to free the ship from the backward drag of the Moon's gravity. But once settled on its course, *Archimedes II* gradually built up to a much higher speed than that: the idea was to reach Venus in a matter of weeks rather than months. For Venus was twenty-six million miles distant in a straight line, and for reasons of fuel economy *Archimedes II* was not following a straight line but a long curve.

So as the great ship drove on through space, indirectly sunwards, the men aboard who were not concerned with running her found plenty of time on their hands.

As on the previous trip, Cliff studied hard to pass examinations in spaceship navigation. Sometimes he took a busman's holiday and plunged into atomic physics, geology, chemistry, agriculture, astronomy and electronics – all subjects of which a top-ranking S.I.D. man was expected to have a fair working knowledge.

Even Magnus did some brushing up on the latest scientific findings.

Doran kept in touch with them by the Visi for some time. But as the ship moved deeper into the fields of electrical disturbances caused by sunspots, interference marred the Visi pictures more and more until they were simply not worth watching. So Doran switched to sound radio only, and reception was passable, though there was always a background crackling of static.

It was by radio he gave the gist of the report issued by the joint expedition to Linné. Bruce, Magnus and Cliff were his audience.

After calling them, he went on: "I judge you're about seven million miles from me now, and it'll take about a quarter of an hour to get an answer from you. So I'll give you the main points all in one go, and wait for your comments later. The Linné parties returned unharmed because there were no Titans to harm them. Repeat, no Titans. At least, not in Linné itself: it was deserted. I've not quite scrapped my idea they may be deep down in the Moon somewhere, but I'm not sold on it any longer.

"From the lower floor in Linné there are several ways down into natural caverns. Most of them are water-filled and all of them seem to wind away endlessly. Perhaps they do lead to a Titan underworld. But I don't know. Only a submarine could get very far through the water-filled ones, and, frankly, my imagination boggles at the size of a sub. needed to carry Titans – and there are a dickens of a lot of narrow bottlenecks. There are no traces of such craft nor of docks for them. So it's on the cards they don't exist.

"The midget submarine, of course, does exist. We – that is, a party from Base Two – salvaged both halves of it. It was rotted by salt water and badly smashed up. Among other things in it, we came across a file of maps of the kind Magnus found. Cross confirms they're sections depicting the vicinity of Linné. So it's a pretty good guess it started out from the caverns below Linné and went all those miles underground before it ran on to that rock and became a wreck.

"The train also exists: twenty sizeable wheeled trucks, and a sort of locomotive driven by a power unit of a kind we also discovered in the sub. We're still investigating that. It seems to contain a battery of extraordinarily long life. We even got the train running, and discovered how to work the elevators.

"But we could only get one particular design of the big machines to work. So far as I could gather, it transforms ordinary lunar rock into a far greater volume of white cement – which is the 'stone' most of the inside of Linné is now composed of. Not cement as we know it, but it pours and sets like cement. Obviously, the Titans used a good many of these machines to fill in and roof over most of the original crater and make a snug Base. When we get the hang of the things properly, we'll soon be building Base Twenty on the Moon, and so begin to get somewhere.

"The swords, tin hats and so forth are real, all right. The swords are sharp enough to shave with – if you could lift 'em. But, like the clubs, they weigh a ton. We're still guessing at the reason for them. The Titans obviously have enough know-how to construct weapons comparable to our vibrator beams, for instance. So why this antique armoury? Breen thinks that to amuse themselves in their pretty bleak outpost the Titans staged gladiatorial combats among themselves, as the Romans did when exiled in Britain and other places. If so, they weren't exchanging love-pats – those things aren't toys.

"Linné as a Base must have been abandoned by the Titans – at least, temporarily. Apart from what I've mentioned, there was little there – no food, clothes, books, pictures, records of any kind. If such things were there to begin with, they've been cleared out now. I expect we'll take it over eventually as Base Three – it's time we had one in that part of the Moon.

"If we make any further discoveries about the whole business, I'll let you know. I hope I've not been fading too badly and you've caught most of this. Acknowledge, and give your comments, if any. Over."

But the comments were few, because Doran had said about all there was to say.

Magnus did ask if any trace of atmosphere, beyond the lunar kind, was found in Linné, and had to wait a quarter of an hour for his voice to carry to Doran and the reply to come, which was simply: "No."

They had a discussion about it afterwards, but it petered out from sheer want of facts. It only led them back to the old speculations about the nature and origin of the Titans. Magnus said jokingly that their home was obvious from their name: they'd come from Titan, the largest of Saturn's many moons.

Bruce pursed his lips and said: "You know, that's not impossible. From what I've seen in my time I've come to believe almost nothing under – or above – the sun is impossible."

Doran came through again every few days, always a little more indistinctly, but had no further light to throw on the mystery of Linné.

And then *Archimedes II* passed the halfway mark to Venus, and the thoughts of the passengers turned more and more to the strange planet as they approached it.

When Kenneth Page had been rescued he was no longer in his right mind. The Venusian who had captured him had kept him in a kind of hypnotic trance while it searched his mind for information about Earth and its inhabitants. Oddly, by some sort of unconscious telepathy, some of the Venusian's own thoughts had drifted into Kenneth's mind and remained there.

And when he rambled, muttering in delirium, sometimes he voiced those thoughts which were not his own. Magnus had recorded them on tape. He had brought the reel of tape with him on this trip, and often played it back while he and Cliff sat listening and brooding over it.

The first and only direct communication men had had from the Venusians was a "thought message" imprinted in a quite mysterious way (though Magnus had hazarded a guess at its operation) upon a small rod. When the rod was held in a bare hand for a short while, the message was slowly transferred to the holder's mind and kept repeating itself. That one terse message told man: "*Our world is our world*." By their actions since, the Venusians had underlined their desire to have no intruding humans near their lake. Plainly, they had written "Unwelcome" on the doormat.

This attitude seemed to them, however, no reason why they shouldn't take a peep at man's world, Earth, and indeed to collect a specimen human to bring home and examine at leisure. And from the evidence on the tape the kidnapping Venusian came to the conclusion that Earth was "no world for us."

After gloomy Venus, Earth's sunlight was far too strong for the creature and half blinded it, for there was no lid to its single eye. Again, the Venusians were fresh-water creatures, and the salt seas of Earth stung the obviously sensitive flesh of the visitor "unbearably." Also, the Venusian learned there were four thousand million humans like the one it had captured, and apparently thought its own kind so drastically outnumbered that they would have little peace or privacy if they came to Earth.

The question now was, what would the Venusians think – and do – when they learned that the humans had decided Venus *was* a world for them?

Archimedes II sped on towards the planet where that question would have to be answered. Venus grew into a well-defined and very bright ball that became bigger and bigger, while Earth had become hard to distinguish from the first magnitude stars, and the Moon was a dust-speck that could be seen properly only through a telescope. The sun had swollen noticeably and the long flames of its prominences writhed slowly about its circumference like the snakes on the head of Medusa.

The whole appearance of the solar system had been altered by the shift of *Archimedes II* in space, but all the stars remained unchanged in their old familiar constellations. They were so immensely far away that to them the voyage of the spaceship was no distance at all.

At last the time came when *Archimedes II*, turned by her flywheels, presented her tail to Venus and squirted a long jet of terribly hot steam at it. The jet slowly grew longer and longer. There was a long fall to brake.

The steam was only slightly radio-active, but it had been decided that it should be employed for braking only outside Venus's atmosphere. If there were living creatures on the surface of the planet, it would scarcely be a diplomatic approach to drench their abodes with radio-active rain. So *Archimedes II* would be slowed almost to a standstill as it entered the atmospheric belt, and the rest of the fall would be retarded by a large and somewhat clumsy appendage packed with chemical rockets.

The skipper was Captain Browne, who had captained the original *Archimedes*, and Cliff did not envy him his job. The recollection of his own bungled landing on the Moon still made him sweat. Venus was a much tougher proposition. Its gravity was roughly equal to Earth's, and so *Archimedes II* would fall with six times the speed and force with which the *Valier* had fallen to the Moon. There would be no horizontal radar screen to help. The visual TV would be almost useless because of the unbroken cloud. There would be the coarse picture from the infra-red TV camera, and there would be the not too accurate radar altimeter. The rest would have to be supplied by the born space-pilot's instinct or sixth sense – and by luck.

Captain Browne had the necessary instinct. It was to be hoped he would have the equally necessary luck.

He took over the controls from the regular pilot. There were twenty men on this ship, and they had come a long way to lay the foundations of Venus Base One. If they could establish a foothold and gain access to a water supply, then on its next trip to Venus *Archimedes II* need carry a propellant tank of only half the size – and so have room to bring near a hundred new members to the colony.

58

All that depended on his landing the vast and weighty ship safely now. And he would have to do it almost blind.

He was a little paler than usual, but calm as a saint. The only other man in the cabin who looked as unworried was Martin Magnus. He was chewing placidly. Bruce looked grim. Cliff clasped his trembling hands behind him so that they wouldn't be noticed. Forgetting that Browne was no raw amateur like himself, he imagined that the Captain was suffering the agonies and misgivings which had torn him not so long ago, and was afraid for him.

So fierce was the thrust from the atomic motor that *Archimedes II* was beginning to halt in her tracks. The ordinary TV screen showed only the dazzling whiteness of the clouds now but twenty miles below. The poor offerings of the infra-red screen were the shadowy marks of mountain ranges, and blurs here and there which were thought to be sizeable vegetation of some kind – maybe forests. The radar screen matched these contours with scarcely more helpful definition. The slowly moving needle of the radar altimeter indicated the falling elevation with seeming confidence, but everyone knew its error could amount to two decameters.

With one decisive twist of his wrist Captain Browne cut the atomic jet completely.

The rotation of the ship to produce artificial gravity had been stopped some time before, and so now *Archimedes II* and all its contents were in a state of free fall. Everyone aboard had been prepared for this and had made themselves fast to suitable fixtures. But they couldn't provide any similar stability for the interior organs of their bodies. The balance cells in their inner ears lost any means of reference. Those men who had had small experience of this kind of thing felt confused and sick. But seasoned space-travellers like the Captain, Beckworth Bruce and Magnus were almost unaffected, and even Cliff had, as part of a S.I.D. man's training, endured many hours in this condition and was able to take it.

It lasted only a matter of seconds.

Then Captain Browne let the battery of chemical rockets open up and forty-eight jets of hot gas joined their forces to resist gravity, and the feeling of weight and direction returned.

The ponderous ship sank slowly into the thickening Venusian atmosphere and presently the clouds seemed to rise to engulf it.

The Captain had a section of the rough radar map of Venus pinned to the console before him. It showed the area chosen for

59

landing, but he rarely glanced at it. He had conned it so often he could see it in his mind's eye, and he was chiefly concerned with manoeuvring the ship so that the picture on the radar screen matched the image in his mind.

It was coming right. The line formation which might be a village or perhaps only a peculiar freak of nature was drifting into the top right-hand corner of the screen. Now it must be held up in that corner so that the ship could land in the apparently uninhabited area which at present covered the centre of the screen.

Captain Browne reached for a control to check the ship's lateral drift.

And then – *Bang!*

Above the muffled roaring of the rocket battery there sounded a a sudden sharp explosion which set everyone's ears ringing. The whole ship, huge as it was, jumped sideways a few yards and lost its balance. The men in the cabin were thrown to the floor, which began to tip steadily to one side. Magnus and Cliff had been flung on their backs. Before they could move, their heads became lower than their heels and momentarily they were as helpless as overturned turtles.

Beckworth Bruce was hunched against the tilting wall, clutching his hairless head: he had crashed it against a bracket and was stunned.

Captain Browne recovered first and crawled grimly on hands and knees up the floor's increasing slope. Somehow, he hauled himself back to the console and began to right the ship.

By the time *Archimedes II* resumed the perpendicular she was very near to the ground and travelling faster than she should be.

Browne looked up at the radar screen. The regular markings which might denote the presence of life had crept down the screen until they occupied more than half of it. If something wasn't done to move the ship laterally she would land among them.

And it was too late to build up any lateral motion at all.

Browne snatched a look at the radar altimeter and at last he displayed alarm. He set his jaw and let the rocket battery go at full blast for a few seconds. Then he switched it off completely, pressed the button which sent the landing shock absorber legs springing out, hung on tightly to the console and, like the rest, hoped for the best.

There came a jarring impact. Cliff shot several inches above the floor and fell back with a painful jolt on his spine. He wasn't the only one to groan. But there was some relief in the groans too. All things considered, the landing wasn't too bad a one. That last spurt from the chemical rockets had saved them from a nasty crash.

But, like Cliff's lunar landing, it was in the wrong place.

The TV screen showed the shaken watchers a view of huts and shacks, in neat lines, just bursting into flame. Red fire grew against the flat grey mist.

And from the huts shadowy, mist-blurred, but remarkably human-looking people were running. From the direction they took, it was plain that they were not merely running from the flames. They were also frightened by the apparition of *Archimedes II*, which had suddenly dropped from nowhere to stand like a giant sentinel over the humble village whose outskirts it had ignited.

Bruce, still holding his aching head with one hand, snatched up a microphone and called over the ship's loudspeaker system: "Attention, the propellant pump crew! Out hose – *now*. Reverse pump. Get out there and do what you can. Don't stop for atmosphere test – it's all right. I want that fire dealt with."

Only seconds after he finished, there came the distant sound of the flexible metallic pipe from the water tank, rattling like a hawser down the side of the ship as the pump crew frantically unwound it. Bruce had kept their fire drill up to the mark. The fiercely hot gases of chemical rockets when a ship landed amid vegetation were prone to set even the greenest leafage and wood ablaze. No one could hope to set up camp in the middle of a forest fire. Hence the emergency scheme of turning the propellant intake pipe into a fire-hose.

But, Doran had warned Bruce, it had to be a real emergency, direly imperilling the ship or its crew. *Archimedes II* had very little water to spare because of the tons needed for the return journey if water was unobtainable on Venus.

Bruce juggled with the direction control of the TV camera until presently he caught in the screen's frame four of the pump crew manhandling the thick and heavy pipe towards the conflagration. One of them signalled back to the ship and water began to trickle from the end of the pipe. Then the pump really got going, and the water came in a fierce, pulsating gush.

Magnus asked Bruce: "Shall Cliff and I go and help?"

"There's only one hose," said Bruce morosely. "You'd only get in the way. They're doing all right."

They certainly were. They were dealing with the fire expertly. They knew there was no water to waste and they were placing every gallon of it in just the right place. But it was a big fire and there were a lot of places to saturate.

Presently, Captain Browne said, without expression: "Shall I check the tank gauge, Mr. Bruce?"

"If I require anyone to do anything, I'll tell them," said Bruce, still morose. "If you're wondering whether we're using too much water, Captain, I can tell you the answer now. We are. Unless we can replace it, we'll never escape from Venus. That, of course, is my responsibility."

"I must point out that I was responsible for the fire," said the Captain, gently.

Bruce raised an eyebrow. "You were responsible for the safety of the ship, and you saved it. You weren't responsible for the explosion which flung it off course."

"I don't know," said the Captain. "I still don't know what went wrong. At a guess, I'd say one of the chemical rockets was faulty and exploded. I checked the whole battery myself before take-off. They seemed all right. But I must have overlooked something. If so, the responsibility rests with me."

Magnus said: "While you two gentlemen fight to take the blame, can Cliff and I go down and take a look at the rocket battery and see if it really was the cause?"

"I seem to be wasting my breath," said Bruce. "A few moments ago I said if I required anyone to do anything –"

"You'd tell 'em," broke in Magnus. "So will you tell Cliff and me –"

"Go – for goodness' sake, go!" snapped Bruce. "You're just bursting to get out there, aren't you?"

"It's stuffy in here," grinned Magnus. "Come on, Cliff."

Archimedes II had fitments denied the smaller, more austere, spaceships. No need this time to drop a ladder from the airlock door and climb dangerously down its swaying length. One just touched a button and a long gangplank, which had fitted snugly into the ship's hull, came swinging down like a narrow drawbridge until its far end rested on the ground below. Then, automatically, it became a simple staircase, with handrails.

Cliff followed Magnus down it, breathing again the heavy, slightly musty, air of Venus. The last time he had set foot on this inhospitable planet he was too worried about the fate of his brother to feel the thrill of first contact with a new world. But this time he was free from care. His feet felt light and tingled with eagerness to explore.

Bruce and the Captain had been too reserved and Magnus too blasé to display excitement over the discovery that a human kind of race existed in the endless mists of Venus. But to Cliff, it was like something in a boys' adventure book. Already he was picturing himself showing the astonished natives films of life on Earth, tasting their queer food dishes, noting down their quaint customs, and writing an adventure book about it himself during the long trip home.

There was no sign of the Venus folk now. The mist had absorbed them.

He and Magnus followed the snaking hose until they caught up with the sweating pump crew. They were just in time to see the last nest of flames doused to charred wood. Blake, the leader of the crew, raised both arms above his head, and the stream of water began to slacken and all at once stopped.

His teeth were very white in his smoke-blackened face as he smiled.

"Hello, Magnus. I hope that's pleased old Bruce. He can't say we wasted any time – or water."

"He didn't look very pleased when we left him," said Magnus. "But I suppose – "

There came a sudden whizz and an ugly plopping sound. Blake's white grin changed to a grimace of agony. He turned and, gasping, began to fall. They saw a short wooden arrow embedded in the base of his neck. Magnus's long arms caught and held him.

The crew exclaimed angrily and stared all about them into the mist. But no one had seen from which direction the arrow came.

Cliff tore off his own jacket and shirt and ripped the latter into rough bandages as Magnus, silent and grim, pulled the arrow out. A spurt of blood followed it, for it had penetrated deeply. But already Blake had fainted.

Cliff rolled one of the shirt strips into a pad and bound it on to the wound, staunching it. The other three men shielded them, standing with their backs to them, glowering at the encircling mist, their fists clenched, for they were weaponless. And still no one had said a word.

There was another whizz, and instinctively Cliff ducked. They all did and the arrow, short and thick, hummed just over their heads. They heard it ping against a tail-fin of the ship and – so silent was everything else – fall with a faint rap on the ground.

Then one of the men bellowed: "There he is!"

Their eyes followed his pointing finger and glimpsed a dim form moving away in the slow eddies of the mist. All three of the pump crew went charging off after it.

"Come back!" shouted Magnus after them.

They were becoming only faint shapes in the mist themselves now, but the crack of command in Magnus's voice halted them in their tracks. Two of them began to return. The other stood irresolute.

"Lamburn – I said come back," called Magnus. "There may be dozens of 'em out there. They know where they are – and you don't."

Gently, he lowered the unconscious Blake to the ground, where Cliff was kneeling.

Lamburn took a pace back towards them, and all at once went sprawling face downwards as if he'd been pushed from behind. The arrow between his shoulder blades was barely visible in the gloomy light.

Cliff bit his lip and resisted the impulse to get up and run. Magnus, however, did run, but in the opposite direction to the one Cliff had contemplated. He pelted like a sprinter over to the stricken Lamburn, passing the other two, who were still dithering.

Lamburn was a heavy man, and Magnus, although tall, by comparison seemed a mere skeleton. Nevertheless, he lifted Lamburn on to his own shoulders as though the big man were hollow, using the grip known as the "fireman's hoist," and began to carry him back.

Cliff wished he could handle Blake as easily. But for one thing he hadn't the strength; and for another, the position of the wound made it imperative to keep Blake's head held up.

The remaining two crew men finally made up their minds. One came back to help Cliff carry Blake. The other – the braver – went to help Magnus.

Trying both to hurry and yet be gentle with their human burdens the four men made their way back towards the ship. Before they reached the gangplank another arrow came whirring among them. Somehow it passed through the centre of the group without touching anyone, though Cliff felt the little wave of displaced air strike his cheek.

"What are they all doing in the ship – just rubbernecking and placing their bets on us?" panted Magnus.

His companions hadn't the breath left to answer. Nor were their minds really on the question. They were all preoccupied by the thought that they had their unprotected backs towards an unseen killer who was taking deliberate pot-shots at them, and they couldn't do a thing about it, not even run away.

Just as they reached the foot of the stairway they had to stop and wait, for down it came clattering swiftly in single file six men, each carrying something which looked like a film camera on a tripod. They recognized the instruments. They were "vibes" – vibrator beam emitters. This gave them heart. It meant that the unknown archers were in for a shock – literally.

Each emitter could put forth for hours at a time a spreading beam of electrical vibrations which, like light, could be focused and its strength varied. It could be damped down until it would give whoever it might play upon nothing worse than an oppressive headache. It could be intensified to shake a man's body so that he couldn't think clearly or perform the simplest action – it would seem to him that he had been seized by a gigantic, invisible hound and was being shaken savagely. And, keyed to its highest pitch, the beam could kill a man in a second by breaking his neck, among other bones.

The six operators began to set up their "vibes" in a semicircle around the bottom of the gangplank, so that the beams would radiate like wheelspokes but widen on the way so that, eventually, they would merge into one wide impassable screen. That screen would stand between the village and *Archimedes II*, and could be moved quickly to stop an attack from any quarter.

Magnus watched them for a moment, and then said solemnly: "My apologies to Baldy and Co."

His gaze dropped to Lamburn's pale face. He scrutinized it, then shoved his hand inside the man's jacket and felt in the region of his heart. At once, he looked concerned. He waved aside the man who had been assisting him, and again lifted Lamburn on to his shoulders. Despite Lamburn's weight, Magnus climbed the narrow stairway as unconcernedly as though he were merely going upstairs to bed.

Bruce and Captain Brown appeared in the doorway at the top, awaiting them.

Cliff made heavier weather of it than Magnus. There wasn't space for two to walk abreast. As Blake's head had to be kept higher than his feet, Cliff was forced to mount the stairs backwards, his arms locked about Blake's chest. Therefore, he had to bear the main weight of the burden. The other fellow could do little to help beyond keeping Blake's feet from bumping against the stairs.

So, sweating, heaving and gasping, Cliff climbed slowly backwards. His feet, which only a short while ago had danced eagerly down these same stairs, now moved falteringly, feeling their way.

Twice he and Magnus had landed on Venus and twice the unfriendly planet had rebuffed them, this time in short order. He recalled the terse thought-rod message from the Venusians of the lake, with its underlying note of warning: *"Our world is our world."*

Man on Venus, it seemed, was fated to be treated not as a friend but as an interloper, an enemy, even by those fashioned in his own shape. Cliff began to feel resentful about it. It appeared to him that the thick Venusian mist was an evil thing. It choked the sunlight, as though that were an interloper also. Perhaps because of that it prevented much of the sun's warmth from reaching the hearts of all the creatures who had to live beneath its heavy canopy.

Far, frozen Pluto could scarcely turn a colder shoulder towards Man's peaceful advances. Cliff felt something harden in his own heart. Man had learnt, at the cost of innumerable terrible wars, to co-operate with himself. He was willing to co-operate with any other reasonable creatures he encountered in this strange universe. But if they rejected him and acted tough, then they were laying up trouble for themselves. For Man, who had conquered the mammoth, the wolves and tigers and the far more dangerous bacteria, had probably garnered more fighting experience than any species this side of Sirius. He could be a good friend – or a ruthless enemy.

With the perspiration running down his face and dripping on the bloodstained shoulder of Blake's jacket, straining and aching, Cliff Page yet made a vow. He would fight alongside Magnus, Bruce, and the rest of them until a human colony was securely established on Venus, whatever the cost, whatever the loss. And he would fight on alone, if necessary.

Then Beckworth Bruce's large hands, out of all proportion to the rest of him, were reaching past him to ease the burden and help lift it back on to the waiting stretcher.

CHAPTER FIVE

THE MYSTERIOUS VILLAGE

The spaceship *Archimedes II*, perhaps the finest single creation of modern science, stood like a besieged Scottish keep in mediaeval times amid the Highland mist. It had withdrawn its defenders behind its walls and raised its drawbridge, and was invulnerable to the stubby arrows which every now and then shot seemingly from nowhere to ricochet from its gleaming sides, which were sheer and unclimbable.

The arrows arrived almost spent, in any case, and obviously were shot from a respectable – and perhaps respectful – distance.

The infra-red camera was not a very satisfactory instrument at any time and it gave the spacemen small help now. It failed to detect any of the archers.

However, while nothing more than wooden arrows were being used against *Archimedes II*, which more than once had withstood the shock of meteors on the journey to Venus, no one inside it was much worried.

But there was the future to think of. They hadn't come to Venus just to remain penned in a spaceship. Sooner or later, *Archimedes II* – somehow – would have to return to Earth, leaving most of them here. What would their situation be then?

After expert treatment by the ship's doctor and surgeon, Blake was already sitting up in his bunk and even joking about his encounter with "that guy playing at Robin Hood", as he described his assailant.

But Lamburn's condition was no joking matter. He was still on the operating table when Beckworth Bruce called a meeting in his tiny private cabin. There were only four of them: Captain Browne, Magnus, Cliff and Bruce himself.

By lighting his big pipe Bruce had conveyed silently that smoking was now permitted on board. Magnus, in hope, had already unpacked his supply of long thin cigars, and was halfway through the first of them. The tobacco haze in the cabin was rivalling the density of the mist outside.

Bruce took his pipe from his mouth and said in his prim, colourless way: "I've called you in here to discuss our next moves. I've reported the situation to Doran. He said he had every confidence in our dealing with it in our own way. So have I. I've a few notions, but I've always thought that four heads are better than one – however good. So I'll be pleased to consider any of your suggestions. We've no clear ideas about what lies out there" – he stabbed with his pipestem towards the porthole – "so let's get straightened out about the facts we do know."

Cliff had long noted that Bruce, probably the world's most famous adventurer, was never one to rush headlong into things. He was a great believer in method and the planned approach. He was not a great talker, and on the rare occasions when he did open up a bit he was apt to become a bore by recounting at length, not his own adventures, but those of Sir John Hunt, a century ago, meticulously planning and then carrying out, stage by stage, the successful assault on the world's highest mountain.

"First," said Bruce, deliberately, "the ship will have to remain here whether we like it or not until we can top up the water tanks. Second, the only known supply of water is the lake our S.I.D. friends here visited. And that's fifty miles away and contains dangerous beasts who know too much about us for my peace of mind. Again, between us and the lake the territory is unexplored, and may harbour all kinds of hazards quite apart from hostile natives of the breed we've already bumped into. Probably we can deal with them, *but* . . . is the lake worth trying for in any case? Remember, the only transport we were able to bring consists of a couple of half-track vehicles with trailers. Using them solely as water carriers, I've reckoned it'll take half a dozen round trips to replace the water we're short of."

"Quite," said Captain Browne. "More, I'd say."

Beckworth Bruce frowned. He disliked the slightest reflection on his accuracy in logistics.

"Six," he said, distantly. "Neither more nor less. I worked it out to three decimal places."

Magnus stepped in to save the Captain's face. "I can't imagine the Venusians letting us dip into their pond once, let alone six times. They have an unpleasant trick of changing the water into acid. Fifty miles is a long way to go to get only a nasty taste in the mouth. Your mathematics may be right, Baldy, but they were – to take it to three decimal places – ninety-nine point nine nine nine per cent a waste of time."

Here Cliff, rightly or wrongly, decided that Bruce's face needed saving, and said hastily: "There must be water nearer than the lake. Where do the natives around here get theirs? I find it hard to believe they fetch it all that way: they're obviously pretty primitive. They would live nearer to the lake if it were the only source. I know the radar maps – so far as they can be trusted – show no other large expanse of water on Venus, but there may be plenty of small streams about."

"That's a point, Page," Bruce admitted.

Magnus said: "All we've actually seen of the natives are some blurred shapes in the mist. They looked human – but were they? Perhaps they don't need water."

"All life needs water," said Cliff.

"Life as *we* know it – so far," said Magnus. "But Mother Nature has a great many surprises in store for us in this universe, and probably on this planet. We don't know what we may run up against – out there."

"Exactly," said Bruce, getting his own back. "That's what I said to begin with. May I remind you, Magnus, we're here to discuss the facts as we know them?"

Magnus examined the glowing end of his cigar, and murmured: "Carry on, Baldy."

The intercom. 'phone buzzed. Bruce answered it. He listened for a few seconds, then said into it: "Well, we can only keep our fingers crossed." He replaced the receiver and told the others: "The operation was successful but blood transfusion is still going on. The Doc gives Lamburn a fifty-fifty chance of pulling round. Well . . . let's get down to business. Where were we?"

"The facts," said Magnus, stonily. Obviously, he was going to be childishly awkward.

"Right, then," said Bruce. "We want water, and we've got to get it from somewhere else but the lake. So, following Page's suggestion, we first try to locate the villagers' supply."

"I'm sure they'll hand it over if we ask 'em nicely," said Magnus, stubbing out his cigar. "Only I was never much good at talking with an arrow through my gizzard."

"The 'vibes' are portable," frowned Bruce. "We have six of them – enough to guard a small party, fore and aft and on both flanks."

Magnus raised an eyebrow. "All marching bravely against one little man with a bow and arrow?"

"Don't be silly, Magnus," said Bruce. "We saw dozens of them streaming from this part of the village, and there must be many more."

"That's right," said Captain Browne, glad of the chance to agree with Bruce.

"We saw dozens of them," said Magnus, "but we've never

seen dozens of arrows come flying our way all at the same time. Not one dozen, not half a dozen, not two arrows. In short, every arrow arrived singly. After that crowd ran away, only one of them was glimpsed again. I'm willing to bet he's solely responsible. He's started a one-man war against us."

"Brave fellow," said Captain Browne.

"Maybe," said Magnus. "He routed us, all right. But he had an important advantage over us: he could see us, whereas we couldn't see him. It's pretty obvious that he can see the ship from wherever he may be now. He's only a bow-shot away, yet even our infra-red camera can't spot him. But, of course, we're not used to this dim light. We weren't born here. He must have different eyes from ours."

"Unless he's using some kind of special optical apparatus," said Cliff.

"People who still use bows and arrows and live in wooden huts are scarcely likely to have such apparatus," said Bruce.

"One would think so, but remember the Titans," said Cliff. "They were well advanced in science and engineering, and yet still used bows and arrows – we saw them. I admit these natives seem to be on a lower level technically, but I'm still puzzling over something. What hit the ship when we were about to land? It might have been some natural force, like lightning, but we've seen no signs of storms. It was an isolated happening. It was much more like an explosion, a deliberate attempt to hit us. It reminds me of those guided missiles – rockets – of old, the things they fired at bombing 'planes in the wars. I wonder if these natives are really so primitive as they appear?"

"Any people still using war rockets are primitive," said Magnus. "But I admit the same thought occurred to me when the bang came. Rushed as we were on our little excursion outside, I still took a good look at the ship's hull. I'll allow I couldn't see the other side of it, but I could see no rents or even scratches made by rocket fragments, and I've checked from the crew that there are no visible penetrations inside. If the natives did fling something like that at us – which I doubt – then they've only themselves to blame for our dropping on to their village."

"I don't think they're to blame," said Captain Browne. "I believe they thought we deliberately fired their village, that we were attacking them. And that's why they hit back at us with the only guided missiles they have – arrows. If they've really got any heavier armament, like rockets, they'd have brought them to bear on us by now."

Cliff had to agree with that.

Magnus also concurred. "I think you're right, skipper."

"I'm happy to agree also," said Bruce, almost genially. "As you know, we haven't any heavy artillery ourselves. The idea of this mission was to bring peace, not a sword. We have only the 'vibes'."

"You're forgetting the fifty reels of blasting tape, Baldy," said Magnus.

Bruce shook his head. "I hope we're never driven to the point of using those as weapons. But perhaps they could be used defensively, to dig our last ditch, as it were. Well, this discussion has cleared the air a bit. We're agreed that we'll dispatch a party to the village to forage for water, and that it's unlikely it'll have to face anything worse than arrows."

"No," said Magnus, "I'm against sending a party. The more men you send, the more lives you risk. Apart from that, it's idiotic to send a whole crowd to discover one simple fact – whether there's water in the village. One man could do that. And I'll be the one man."

"It's incredible!" exclaimed Bruce. "You say that, and yet you saw what happened to Lamburn and Blake right in front of your eyes?"

"It wouldn't have happened if they'd been wearing suits of armour. Make no mistake – I'm going armed, with a 'vibe', and armoured too."

"Armoured?" They all said it.

"Of course," said Magnus. "In a spacesuit."

"Of course," echoed Cliff, remembering the suits Magnus meant. It was known that spacesuits were unnecessary on Venus, and so none had been brought for wear there. But occasionally – very rarely – it was necessary to effect minor outside repairs to the ship while it was travelling through space, such as sealing a dangerous meteor rent or adjusting a jammed exterior TV camera. Then an engineer – or perhaps two – would exit through the airlock but remain attached to the ship by cables to prevent their drifting away, and carry out the repairs.

The spacesuits they wore were very similar to the standard lunar spacesuit, except that they had no lead soles to weight them.

Of course, the men did not "fall", as they stepped out of the airlock, because they were travelling at exactly the same speed as the ship itself and there was no air resistance to tear them away from it. Also, the ship's own mass provided the strongest gravitational pull in the immediate vicinity, and "down" was towards the ship.

But the ship's spin around its longitudinal axis had to be stopped, temporarily, for the duration of the task, else the men would have been flung away from the ship by centrifugal force.

The suits were of stout metal – jointed, indeed, like suits of armour and polished on the outside. They had to stand up to extremes of temperature, for in space only half of the ship's hull would likely be in sunlight and the other half in shadow.

The face-plate of each suit was of darkened quartz to cut down the ultra-violet rays, but not so dark as to blindfold the wearer when in shadow. So an adjustable metal visor, like the peak of a cap, was set just above the face-plate to shield the eyes further in direct sunlight.

Cliff also remembered that there were only two suits on board, and put in his claim quickly. "I'll come with you, Magnus."

Magnus grinned at him. "If you want to."

Bruce said, heavily: "Go ahead, make your own arrangements. Don't mind me – I'm only supposed to be running this show."

"This sort of job is what we're trained for and what we came for," said Magnus. "Don't worry, we shan't just disappear into the blue without a word. The suits are fitted with radio, you know. We'll inform you of everything we see, and if anything goes wrong you'll be the wiser for our information – and our mistakes. Then every year you can lay flowers in front of our memorial tablet in the S.B. building, muttering 'I warned 'em, but they wouldn't listen'."

"I shouldn't waste the money," said Bruce, brutally. He sat sucking at his pipe for a while. "All right," he said, suddenly. "Get into your fancy dress."

*

It was far from easy to walk in the "fancy dress". One could bounce along merrily on the Moon in a spacesuit or float around happily in one in space. But under Venusian gravity they weighed heavily on the wearer, despite Magnus having removed the large oxygen cylinders and breathing apparatus. He had also removed the darkened face-plates, since it was almost impossible to see through them in this weak light.

The absence of the face-plates allowed the pair to breathe the Venusian air directly and speak to each other, but also it left a narrow gap vulnerable to a well-aimed arrow. However, they

72

lessened this chink in their armour by pulling their visors well down, leaving a mere slit for them to see through.

But it was hot and close inside the suits, and the perspiration seemed to run from every pore.

More than ever there was a mediaeval atmosphere about things as Magnus and Cliff clanked down the drawbridge like knights going out to do battle. And, in fact, they were doing just that.

They watched the gangplank rise slowly behind them and merge into the tall ship's side. Cliff clutched his "vibe" more tightly and hoped their deduction had been right about the comparative harmlessness of the natives. Then they lumbered awkwardly towards the scorched village.

The destruction covered only a small area, but then, the village was not all that large. The wooden shacks had no glass in the windows, and there was no evidence that the inhabitants – who seemed to have fled their homes without exception – even knew what glass was. Everything was quite primitive. There was earthen pottery, mats of coarse grass, and rough wooden tables and stools.

In some of the huts there were spears and bows leaning in corners.

It was all remarkably similar to any one of a hundred villages in the few, but still existing, backward areas of Earth.

Magnus conscientiously reported it all to Bruce through his suit's built-in walkie-talkie set.

Soon, they emerged into a square open space of beaten earth which appeared to be the village centre and general gathering place. Plumb in the middle of it was a large circular pool, some seven or eight yards in diameter, full of clear water. There was an artificial rim to it about a foot high. And that rim was of bright, untarnished metal that looked like stainless steel.

Cliff and Magnus stared at it and then glanced significantly at each other through their helmet slits.

"This," said Magnus, "needs prompt investigation."

"What does?" asked Bruce's voice, sounding metallic and somehow plaintive through the tiny loudspeakers.

"We've found an oasis," explained Magnus. "Hold on a moment, Baldy."

A closer inspection was even more surprising. The whole pool was of metal, smooth-surfaced, a shining pan let into the bare earth. It was some six feet deep in the centre, and there was a hole there in the bottom like the wastepipe of a washbowl. The water

73

was as transparent and still as crystal and reached to within a few inches of the gleaming rim.

They walked slowly around it, peering into it from different angles. Magnus all the while describing it to Bruce. It was difficult through the slits to see just where one was putting one's feet, and Cliff stumbled over something and almost went headlong into the pool. He stopped to examine the something. It was a cubic box, also of metal, let into the rim. On top of it was a single knob with a pointer. A few graduation marks were engraved in a semi-circle about it.

Magnus inspected it too.

"Nicely made," he commented. "Fine craftsmanship. Nothing like the crude work of the local inhabitants. A puzzle box, eh, Cliff?"

Then, of course, he had to satisfy the curiosity of the impatient, listening Bruce.

Cliff gripped the knob with his metal-clad fingers. "Shall I give it a whirl?"

"Sure – but just a moment. Listen, Baldy, we're having a shot at finding out what this knob does. Maybe it'll sound an alarm and bring a fire-engine. Or maybe it'll just blow us to dust. If you don't hear from us afterwards, then look out of the porthole and you may see us blowing past you on the wind. In that event, you'll know enough to leave Pandora's box alone."

"Goodbye, boys," was Bruce's brief and heartless response.

Cliff turned the knob one graduation. Nothing appeared to happen, so he turned it another couple.

"Look," said Magnus. "The water level is rising."

It was. Slowly, the water line crept up towards the top of the rim.

"Stop it," said Magnus, "or it'll spill over and we'll get rusty feet."

Cliff stopped it.

"Simple enough," said Magnus. "That hole down there is the inlet, not the outlet. The natives help themselves to all they want and then just top up the pool again with this gadget. It's a valve control. So it's all laid on for them. But who laid it on?"

Cliff had no answer, but looked keenly all round the clearing, peering down the narrow, straight streets to the point where they dissolved away into the mist. And still the village appeared to be completely deserted.

"Let's wander on," said Magnus. They did so, choosing a street down which they could see the dim outline of a hut much bigger than any they had come across so far. As they approached it, they saw the doorway was unusually large.

"This must be the headman's house," said Magnus, looking keenly at the dark doorway. "If he isn't in, let's leave our visiting cards."

They both held their vibrators levelled as they entered. The great barn-like place was empty of living things, but the sight of the ordered array of inanimate things set them back on their heels with astonishment.

"Confusion worse confounded," said Magnus, inevitably.

The light from the windows, which again were merely cut-out holes, was feeble, but it was quite enough to enable them to recognize the assortment of giant weapons. There were huge steel swords, some in scabbards; spiked clubs that dwarfed them; a couple of helmets each big enough to boil a sheep in; spears which ran the whole length of the hut; a metal bow fifteen feet tall leaning against one wall; and a heap of wooden arrows, thick as broomsticks.

Once again they were back in the fairy-tale land of Linné.

But there was no furniture in the hut, none of the huge stone chairs and tables – indeed, there was no room for them.

Magnus said slowly, for Bruce's benefit: "We seem to have walked into a Titan's private house. Yes, one of the Titans of Linné. He's not at home just now and I hope he's gone out for a nice long walk. I wonder how we get to the beanstalk from here?"

He told Cliff to keep watch at the door and went on to describe the place they were in.

Bruce commented: "Well, this is an eye-opener, to be sure. I think it proves the Titans aren't a lunar race, after all. They must come from Venus. I expect they constructed that pool you saw. At least, one of them did. Perhaps there's only one in every village. Perhaps he's in charge of the village – the headman, the boss. What do you think?"

"I just don't know what to think," said Magnus. "There's no furniture in this house, and if there were he couldn't possibly get into it. I don't think he can actually live here – maybe he's got a bigger place up the road. This one strikes me as merely an armoury – nothing more."

Cliff, at the door, was wondering if the giant *did* return, and if he was in no friendly mood, whether their "vibes" would give the monster even as much as a headache. Then he jumped as a loud, metallic clatter came from just behind him. In lively alarm, he turned and saw that Magnus had yanked at the great bow and caused it to fall to the floor.

Magnus planted both feet on the centre, or handgrip, of the bow, and pulled upwards with both hands at the steel wire which served as its cord. He strained and grunted, trying to bend the thing. He succeeded. He bent the bow exactly one inch, and then, almost collapsing, had to let it go.

"Gosh!" he panted. "If the Titans can handle these things, then I'll be careful to mind my 'p's' and 'q's' if I ever speak to one. I'll be so polite it'll hurt."

Cliff picked up one of the arrows. There was a wicked-looking steel barb at the business end, sharp as a pin. The "feathers" were metal vanes.

He said: "So we've nothing to fear except a few arrows, eh? Just one of these from a bow like that would skewer us together, spacesuits and all!"

"Time we moved on," said Magnus at once.

They went farther along the street, but there were no more big huts and the smaller variety began to thin out.

"We're coming to the far end of the village," Magnus informed Bruce.

"Better turn back, then," said Bruce. "We've found what we want, although I don't know whether there'll be enough of it. It depends upon the volume of the main source of the water. I'll send one half-track along with tanks and a pump, to begin with. We'll see how it goes."

"Right," said Magnus.

Cliff had wandered on some yards to the very last shack and was staring aimlessly around at a mist-bound patch of open land that contained nothing but the coarse grass which apparently surrounded the village. At least, so he thought, until he noticed something not quite ordinary. Near to where the wall of mist stood, on the far side of the patch, there were two straight parallel lines where the grass didn't grow. They were about a yard apart, running away from him, away into the mist.

At once, he suspected what they might be. But he called Magnus.

Magnus had the same idea. "Train lines?" he said.

They walked over to them, and there were the familiar grooves of the kind they had followed down the long spiral path in the crater of Linné. Only this time the hard white stone was set firm in grassy soil.

They followed them, and twenty yards farther on came upon

76

the train itself, standing stationary on the line, unattended. It was like the one described to them over the radio by Doran, a score of open trucks headed by quite a small locomotive, which hid its secrets beneath a seamless container.

In fact, it was little more than a box on wheels, with a cockpit for the driver which contained one seat and the controls. The controls were simplicity itself: one panel in which were set three buttons. The same parsimoniousness with press buttons which had been noticeable in Linné was also evident here.

All the trucks were loaded with tree trunks of all sizes, stripped and trimmed, though not very neatly: either the tree-fellers had had blunt axes or else they had been in a tearing hurry to get this load finished.

The two men from Earth walked along the length of the train, examining it.

Cliff was feeling very tired. Dragging about in the heavy suit had sapped a great deal of his energy. When they stopped at the locomotive, he merely leant against it while Magnus studied the cockpit. Presently, Magnus turned away and flung his arms wide in a gesture of defeat. He was tired too – it showed in his eyes – and his eyebrows were beaded with sweat.

"This," he said, "is one of the occasions when I yearn for Sycamore Lane, an armchair by the fireside, a good book and a dry martini – where everything is sane and orderly and far removed from crazy things like this."

Martin Magnus had a house in Sycamore Lane, in London, and it was his refuge from the world and all other worlds when he could get to it.

He told Bruce about the train, adding despairingly: "Don't ask me what it all adds up to, how it all fits together. The village natives couldn't have built this railway, surely? If the Titans did, then why did they make it so small? This must be like a toy train to them. If they can build trains, why do they play around with crude, obsolete weapons? The evidence keeps contradicting itself. I'm going crazy trying to figure it out."

"Don't worry, it'll keep," said Bruce. "You've done enough. Come on back now. The half-track is just setting out to the pool. Look in on them on the way back and show them how that valve control works if they have any trouble."

"I'm not coming back with only half the answers," said Magnus, stubbornly. "I want to know where this train goes to. Maybe I'll be able to get some chewing gum on the next station platform."

Cliff's heart sank. He'd really had enough. But he wouldn't admit it to Magnus for the world. S.I.D. men were expected to go on until they could go no farther – and then go on from there. He summoned a smile, which Magnus couldn't see anyway.

"Which button shall we push?" he said, bravely.

They turned deaf ears to Bruce's protestations and climbed on to the locomotive. There was room for only one of them in the cockpit and Magnus got there first. Cliff had to lie awkwardly – because one couldn't sit in these stiff suits – on the engine covering.

Magnus prodded the button on the left. Smoothly and silently the train began to run backwards.

"Whoops!" exclaimed Magnus, and pressed the middle button. It was a lucky choice. The train braked as smoothly as it had started, and from where he was Cliff judged the rearmost truck had stopped only a couple of yards from where the track ended.

"So it must be this one," said Magnus, pushing the remaining button. The simple deduction was correct. The train glided forwards, picking up speed. Whatever motor powered it made not the slightest hum, and the only sound was the faint grinding of the metal wheels on the smooth stone. When the train started there was a brief clinking of couplings – no louder than the rattle of tea-cups – and then they were heard from no more. Obviously, the designers had respected efficiency.

Cliff turned with difficulty to see where they were going, but it was largely wasted effort. The wall of cloud-mist kept its distance from them, never allowing them a sight of more than twenty yards or so of the line ahead. The unchanging carpet-pattern of spiky grass unrolled on either side.

It was all rather unnerving. Cliff kept wondering: supposing there was an obstruction on the line, would they see it in time to pull up? He wished he knew where they were going. Supposing there was another train coming towards them on this single line? He cursed the mist.

Again, he wondered if they were being watched. Behind the walls of mist flanking their progress hundreds of eyes stronger than theirs might be regarding them, hating them.

And then there were the Titans. If they came striding out of the mist . . .

All at once he noticed a change in the monotonous scenery. The grassy area on the right began to slope down, away from the line, until it seemed, as one looked only that way, the train was running along the top of an old-fashioned railway embankment.

Then quite suddenly the slope was dirty grey and black, grassless, rough, and pitted with diggings.

"Hello," said Magnus. "What's this?" He stopped the train.

"Mineral workings," said Cliff, surveying what was visible of them, for the slope ran pretty steeply down into the ubiquitous mist. "Looks like iron ore to me. I expect this is where the natives get the iron for tipping their arrows."

"Perhaps," said Magnus. "But, if so, they must make an industry of it and supply all the other villages – they've been digging like mad: it can't be just for their own needs. Let's go down and have a look."

"Right," said Cliff. He tried to say it cheerfully, but it didn't quite come out that way. The inexplicability of everything they came across, the silence, the forbidding, ever-present mist, the absence of any friendly life, such as birds or animals, and the stifling, tiresome metal suit all combined to depress him. He wondered if he had made a mistake in joining the S.I.D. Perhaps he wasn't temperamentally suited to it. Surely he had been happier in his former post as a minor marine biologist at Plymouth?

He began to understand Martin Magnus's dislike – and sometimes expressed fear – of all the lonely tracts of space and alien lands which lay far beyond Earth's comfortable atmospheric belt.

Then he remembered his vow to see this thing through, and began to shuffle grimly after Magnus down the slope. There could be no turning back now. He told himself it was only a mood.

It soon became clear that the diggings were no mere surface scratches. This slope wasn't natural. It was part of a great pit – the size of which probably they would never learn – scooped out in search of the iron ore. In contrast to the neat, efficient train the implements used here were primitive. Here and there they stumbled on spades with long wooden handles and blunt picks of inferior metal.

They examined them and described them to Bruce, who commented: "All I can say is 'Confusion worse confounded'."

"That's copyrighted," protested Magnus.

"Listen!" said Cliff, suddenly.

Magnus was too experienced and wary to query such a request. Instinctively, at the first hint of danger, he froze. Bruce was an old hunter too. He remained silent. The only sound anywhere was the faint wash of the carrier wave from the little loudspeakers.

Then Cliff heard the other sound again, and Magnus for the

79

first time: a low whispering of several voices carrying clearly in the still air.

And then, like a cloud of attacking hornets, a volley of stubby arrows came humming at them. Half of them missed altogether. The rest went glancing and bouncing off their armoured forms in a brief, wild dance.

Automatically, they pressed the buttons of their "vibes", spraying the invisible electronic beams in the general direction of their equally invisible foes. There was a chorus of thin shuddering shrieks, away in the mist. They were pitiful to hear, but Magnus and Cliff grimly kept the radiation on for another five seconds, for that was the limit of human endurance before the vibrations shook the last of consciousness from their victims. They had to assume that their attackers were that much human.

Then: "The natives are on the warpath," Magnus told Bruce. "They've just loosed a broadside of arrows at us. I think the 'vibes' have settled 'em for a bit. Anyhow, we're going in for a close look."

"This," said Bruce, "is interesting. See if you can collect a specimen. We've got to find out who these people are and what everything's about. We'll get nowhere by guessing. But watch your step."

"You bet," said Magnus, tersely.

They went, treading carefully, slantwise down the slope towards the origin of the arrows and cries. The mist-wall retreated as steadily before them and gradually revealed its secrets. Nearly forty natives lay motionless in various attitudes on the ground, some still clutching their bows, some with bows and spilled arrows lying beside them.

"Human," said Magnus, quietly. "Or near enough."

They were scantily dressed, each with a single garment from waist to thighs, composed of stout, broad, green leaves tacked together. Although many of them looked quite young, all of them, without exception, had a shock of white hair which began low on their foreheads. Their skin was unnaturally white also, like that of albinos. Their noses were hooked, their pale lips thin, their ears pointed like those of elves. They were gaunt-looking creatures.

All were in deep unconsciousness but not a single face was serene. Oblivious as they were, still they frowned, with down-drawn mouths, looking stern and cruel.

Despite the numbing warmth of his suit, Cliff felt a little shiver go over him. These were typical children of Venus, which was

80

called in Earth's mythology "the planet of love", but in fact so far had shown them nothing but antagonism.

Impersonally, as though these were laboratory specimens, Magnus described their appearance to Bruce.

"H'm," said Bruce. "Let's hope their aspect belies them. I'd rather co-operate, but if they don't understand the meaning of the word we'll just have to get tough with them."

Cliff, who was staring around, said: "Wait a bit – there's some more yonder."

About twenty yards beyond this group, at the edge of the mist, other still forms were only just visible. They went on to look at them and found there were plenty of them – indeed, nearly a hundred. And they were all women and children, and all quite unconscious.

"Perhaps we were a bit hard on them," said Magnus. "The men were out in advance of their women-folk and children, guarding and shielding them. There are still some tribes on Earth who, in these circumstances, would have placed the women between themselves and danger. I'm beginning to take a slightly kindlier view of them, Baldy. At least, they're men."

"Speaking for myself –" began Bruce, and then the flat, twanging reproduction of his voice was drowned in a wild yelling, horrible to hear.

Magnus and Cliff turned to see a flying wedge of natives burst from the mist and come across the slope towards them at a staggering, lopsided run. They had slung their bows and were wielding long, thin spears. Cliff went cold at the sight of them. Arrows were hit or miss affairs, but the thought of one of those spears thrust deliberately though the narrow aperture of his helmet ...

The picture seemed to hypnotize him. His thoughts refused to move. He completely forgot the vibrator in his hand. He stood there like a fool, just staring at the rushing, nearing throng.

The leading man, who was well out in front, was a wild-eyed fellow, taller and even thinner than the others. His look was murderous and fixed on Cliff, and as he ran he drew back his spear for a throw.

CHAPTER SIX

ENTER ARGEN

But Magnus got there first with his "vibe."

The leader reeled, overcome by convulsive tremors. He dropped his spear in his agony and then crumpled on top of it, writhing. His followers fell also, their heads jerking as though they were in an epileptic fit. Some rolled, kicking helplessly, down the slope. Others fell ungracefully into the excavations. They cried out briefly, and then were silent, for the vibrations paralysed their vocal cords.

The leader, being the nearest, had received the strongest shock from Magnus's vibrator, switched to low power though it was. Yet he was the last to cease twitching and lie as still as the others.

Magnus regarded him approvingly. "He's the toughest of the bunch – probably the top man. We'll take him. But keep your eyes skinned for any more surprise attacks. We nearly fell for this one."

Cliff said: "If it hadn't been for you, we should have. I was scared useless."

When they lifted the tall native they found that, although sinewy, he was surprisingly light.

"Their bones can't be very strong," said Magnus. "Be careful with him."

At once Cliff became very conscious of his stiffly metal-clad fingers. They were liable to pinch and break delicate things – it wasn't easy to control the joints. However, he was as gentle as he could be as they toiled back up the slope to the train, carrying the native between them. He was tired to begin with, and this extra exertion became almost unbearable. Inside he was crying silently for the chance to get to some place where they could remove their suits and lie down and rest. But this was not the place to do either. The knocked-out natives would soon be recovering their senses.

The last straw was that Bruce kept nagging at them over the radio, demanding to be "put in the picture."

Magnus said, gaspingly: "For heaven's sake . . . Baldy . . . wait . . . will you?"

They laid the native face-downwards on the engine covering,

and Cliff had to lie beside him, grasping the man's arms behind his back, for they had nothing to secure him with. Magnus resumed his place in the driving cockpit and jabbed the left-hand button. The train went gliding backwards.

Only then did Magnus bring Bruce up to date about what had happened. It was a longish story.

"Nice work," Bruce approved. "Now we're getting somewhere."

Cheered, Magnus started his old formula. "Put the kettle on to boil – "

At which moment it became apparent that they'd got somewhere sooner than they had expected. There was nothing to mark where the track ended, and they were at the wrong end of the train to see clearly just where the furthermost truck was getting to. And the mist didn't help.

With most of his attention on satisfying the impatient Bruce, Magnus had misjudged the distance they had to return. The trucks at the far end rode off the track on to the grass, became disjointed and piled up noisily on one another. The tree trunks fell off at all angles and added to the jam.

The locomotive, sturdily trying to back itself into this confusion, reared itself up like a bucking horse, nose down, rear in the air. Cliff and the native slid right off it. Magnus pitched head-first from the cockpit.

Cliff lost his grip on his captive who, until then, hadn't moved a muscle. Now he moved plenty. He sprang up like a bouncing ball and raced off into the mist, white hair streaming behind, back in the direction they had come from. Cliff, lying with the chin of his helmet digging into the ground, didn't attempt pursuit. Even if he hadn't been encumbered with the suit, he was so weary that it would have been hopeless.

The engine had toppled to one side, and rested at an absurd angle, its wheels still turning. Magnus scrambled to his feet and reached into the cockpit to switch it off.

Cliff got up a deal slower. They stood there looking at the mess.

"All right, I'll say it," said Cliff. "Confusion . . . worse . . . confounded."

"How right you are," said Magnus, gloomily, and then snarled into his microphone: "Oh, be quiet, Baldy, you cackling old hen! If you'd stopped nagging for just two minutes together, this would never have happened."

"What wouldn't have happened?" asked Bruce, coldly, and

became heated when he was told. Magnus switched his radio set off, and Cliff had to bear with the old man's recriminations.

They trudged heavily back to the village, through the still empty streets, and came out into the main square. But this was now populated to some extent.

A half-track vehicle with a trailer, both loaded with huge water tanks, stood beside the pool. Four men stood around it, carrying "vibes," and obviously guarding it. An electric pump sprouting two pipes, one leading into a tank and the other into the pool, also stood there, but no one was attending to it.

The guards raised their vibrators in salutation.

"Seen any Indians?" asked one.

"Plenty," said Magnus. "Too many. Heap big ones. About a mile the other side of the village. The whole population of this hick town, I'd guess."

"Friendly?"

"Friendly! They darn nearly had our scalps," answered Magnus, looking into the pool. "Hi, what's going on here?"

There wasn't a drop of water in the big, gleaming bowl. Instead, there were two men standing in it, pushing the end of the pipe down the central hole. They looked up.

"We've emptied the pool once," one of them said, "but we've still got room for some more in the tanks. Only the spring seems to have dried up."

Cliff pointed to the valve-control box. "Didn't Bruce tell you how to work that?"

"He told us how it was *supposed* to work," said the man. "But it doesn't. Not for us, anyway."

Cliff walked round to the box and juggled with the knob.

"Take out that darned pipe," Magnus directed, and the men did so. Cliff expected the water to follow it, but it didn't. He waited. They all waited. And nothing at all came from the central hole. Cliff began to feel somewhat foolish. Magnus came round and moved the knob this way and then that. He wasn't lucky either.

He muttered something that sounded fierce, but it was muffled by his helmet. He removed his helmet and repeated what he'd said and it was certainly fierce enough. He began to get out of his suit altogether.

"No need for these any longer," he said to Cliff. "We have six 'vibes' here now – enough to settle a thousand natives."

Cliff was only too glad to agree. Indeed, he was so anxious to have done with his suit that he shed the last portion of it

84

before Magnus was clear of his. He felt stones lighter, and drew in great draughts of air. The tiredness began to go.

Magnus joined the men in the centre of the metal pool, peered down the hole and then thrust his arm down it. When he withdrew it, the sleeve was still dry.

He frowned, said nothing, and came back to his discarded spacesuit. He switched on the little set again and reported this latest disappointment to Bruce.

"This is like a game of snakes and ladders," commented Bruce. "We've come down a couple of snakes and we're just about back where we started from. You'd better make it a complete reversal and come right back where you started from. Come home – all is forgiven."

So they went back to *Archimedes II*, perched insecurely on the overloaded half-track.

After refreshment, which in fact was tea, there was another conference in Beckworth Bruce's cabin to scheme the next step. The same quartet was present.

Bruce was for moving into the empty village and taking it over. He sketched out a plan for six guard posts, each armed with a vibrator and manned by three men on duty in shifts, covering every approach to the village. They would be linked by radio and also in touch with a central command post which he intended to set up by the pool in the square. He proposed uprooting the pool altogether and excavating to see if they could tap the underground pipe which supplied it.

As usual, he wanted their comments before he made the day's report to Doran.

Cliff asked: "What about the natives? Where will they live meantime?"

"That's their affair," said Bruce, firmly. "I don't like to be harsh with them. If we can come to terms with them no one will be more pleased than I. But they've got to learn to keep their fingers off their bow-strings. Lamburn is still hovering between life and death, and I'm not a bit happy about it. If it comes to that, I wasn't pleased at their attempts to spear you two, although you've only yourselves to blame for that – I told you not to go off on that joy-ride."

They talked for quite a bit longer, and at length decided that – with Doran's endorsement – Bruce's plan should be adopted.

And then, such being the way of life, all their talk was rendered pointless and their plan shredded to pieces by a new and unexpected turn to events.

85

The man who was on duty in the control cabin, watching the TV and infra-red screens, reported on the intercom: "There's a bunch of natives approaching from the village, sir. I don't think it's an attack. So far as I can see, they're unarmed. But they're carrying a man."

The conference broke up at once. The four of them crowded to the porthole.

The short Venusian day – it was approximately only twelve hours long – was ending and it was getting dark outside. Despite that, and despite Bruce's bald head blocking half the porthole before him, Cliff saw the natives reasonably clearly. There were five of them, clustered together. One was out in front a couple of paces bearing aloft the branch of a tree, thick with the same sort of leaves which composed their garments. Cliff guessed it was a kind of flag of truce – the equivalent of an olive branch on Earth.

Behind the branch bearer, the remaining four carried the inert body of another native.

"Shall we 'vibe' them, sir?" came the duty man's voice from the speaker on the desk.

"No!" snapped Bruce.

The group halted near the point where the gangplank, when it was down, touched the ground. They dropped their burden without ceremony. The leader cast down his branch on top of it, and then the five of them turned and went racing away, their long, thin limbs moving rapidly at almost comical angles. The gathering gloom swallowed them.

The form on the ground rolled over, dislodging the branch, but did not rise.

"He's bound hand and foot," said Magnus, suddenly. "I think they've offered us a sacrifice."

The prudent Captain Browne muttered something about it being perhaps a trap.

Bruce didn't even answer him. "Down gangplank," he said into the intercom. "Send two men to bring that native in. Fetch him to my cabin. Send another man with them to act as guard, with a 'vibe'."

"Yes, sir."

It was no trap. The men brought the trussed native up the gangplank without interference. Within a few minutes, there was a knock at the door and the men bundled in and deposited their load as if they were merely delivering a parcel.

"Good heavens, it's old Spear-'em-Quick!" exclaimed Magnus.

86

"Who?" frowned Bruce.

But Magnus was bending over the new arrival.

"It's the leader of the bunch who attacked us – the fellow who got away," explained Cliff.

The native was fully conscious now, but just as helpless as though he were not. His hands were tied behind him and his legs bound together with what looked like plaited creeper. His mouth was still down-turned grimly. And his eyes were still wild-looking and stared round at them as though he would like to kill them all if he could. The irises were pale, almost colourless. Cliff wondered if this general lack of pigmentation in the natives were because of the equivalent lack of sunlight.

"It's full circle again," said Magnus, beginning to untie the bonds. "Or, if you like, Baldy, we've gone up a ladder."

"Hold on," said the Captain, disturbed. "Is it wise to free him?"

"I think four of us should be able to handle him," said Magnus, sarcastically.

Bruce settled himself at his desk. He moved a heavy paper-weight nearer, so that it was handy in case of emergency, and said, at his most urbane: "You have a reputation, Magnus, for picking up foreign lingoes very quickly. Let's see if you can get anywhere with our guest."

"It depends whether he feels like talking," said Magnus, re-moving the last strand of the creeper. He stood back.

The tall native sat there on the floor, rubbing his skinny wrists. Magnus motioned to him to rise. He did so, slowly, towering over them, yet so fragile-seeming that they didn't feel too uneasy.

"It's always best to make the first approach through the stomach," said Magnus. "Have the cook send up some assorted food, but mainly vegetables."

"You think they're vegetarians?" asked Bruce.

"I don't know, but I haven't seen any animals around. But, of course, they might be cannibals . . ."

"Ugh!" shuddered Bruce. He sent for the food.

When it came, Magnus arranged a dish of potatoes, carrots and onions. He took trouble over it, apparently trying to make it look appetizing. He held it out to the native, who merely stood there and gave no hint that his palate had been tickled.

Magnus tried a friendly grin. "Take it," he said, offering it again.

The native took it, and promptly threw it straight in Magnus's face.

Cliff laughed aloud, Bruce gave a dry chuckle, and even Captain Browne gave a slightly puzzled smile. Magnus's grin had gone, but he remained calm. He picked pieces of carrot from his untidy mop of hair and said: "I've had this happen before. He probably thought it was poisoned. This is going to take a lot of patience, but you'll see . . ."

He began at the beginning, pointing a finger at his chest and saying: "I – man. You – ?"

The others sat around watching until at last the native's reserve or patience broke, and he pointed a finger at his own chest, on which every rib was visible, and made a throaty noise which sounded like "Argen" – with a hard "g."

"Glad to know you, Argen," said Magnus, and his grin returned.

"Is that his proper name, the name of his tribe, or of his species?" asked Bruce.

"How the dickens do I know?" said Magnus. "Give me time."

They gave him a lot of time. Bruce spent most of it making a report to Doran. After almost an hour, the native was sitting comfortably on a chair, indicating that he'd like some more potato, and had smiled twice. But all Magnus had learned was that Argen was his personal name, his tribe was the "Bamu," the village was called "Lomba," and food was "munch" – which, as Magnus pointed out, was easy to remember.

Cliff was becoming tired again, and this time it was through need of sleep. Bruce and Captain Browne admitted to weariness also.

"All right," said Magnus. "You three go and get some sleep. Argen and I are getting on fine, but I think it's going to be an all-night session. You'll let us have the use of your cabin for the night, Baldy?"

"But where am I going to sleep?" objected Bruce, looking longingly at his bunk.

"There are spare camp-beds in the quartermaster's store," said Magnus. "I must have some privacy if I'm going to get anywhere with Argen. Your snores wouldn't help at all."

Bruce went with bad grace. Despite his age, or perhaps because of it, sometimes he could be as petulant as Magnus himself. Cliff and the Captain selfishly went to their own comfortable bunks.

*

In the grey Venusian dawn Bruce returned to his cabin. He was disgusted to find Argen curled up in his bunk, fast asleep.

Magnus was writing at the desk. He had filled several sheets, which lay on the desk beside a tape-recorder. His eyes were a little bloodshot and he looked even more sallow than usual.

He asked: "Are Cliff and the Captain up yet?"

"I don't know," mumbled Bruce.

Magnus said nothing but his look said plainly: "Go and see." Bruce went, and Magnus resumed writing.

When they were all crowded in the little cabin again, Magnus began: "Although I say it myself, it's been a good night's work. I've written out for general use an English-Bamu dictionary of basic words. I've spelt the Bamu words phonetically and listed their English counterparts – or rough counterparts – beside them. Additionally, I've recorded them on the tape, with Argen saying the words – in this same order – and myself repeating them directly afterwards in English. And I've written quite a treatise on the grammar, which is fairly simple, thank heavens. Using that little lot, I see no reason why all of you shouldn't be able to speak pidgin Bamu in a few days."

"Good," said Bruce. "Doran will be pleased."

"Yes, he'll probably be decorated for it," said Magnus, with a trace of bitterness.

"Have you learnt anything about the Titans?" asked Cliff, eagerly.

"The Titans – ah!" said Magnus. "Yes, I pumped Argen about them. They exist, all right. Only – under another name. They're called 'Meks.' Does that ring a bell with you, Cliff?"

"Meks?" Cliff pondered, and then an incident from the past returned vividly to him. He said: "I don't know if this is the connection, but I remember when we were bringing Ken back from Venus he mumbled a word in his sleep. It meant nothing to us, and we guessed he'd got it from the Venusian's mind. It was 'Mekmen'."

"That's it," said Magnus. "We wondered whether it was the name of some person, or whether it meant 'Mek Men.' Actually, he'd got the name 'Mek' and also the hazy idea that the Meks were men. Hence, 'Mek Men'."

"But the Venusians are jellyfish, water creatures, and the Meks are giants who must live on land," said Bruce, slowly. "What possible connection can they have?"

"Argen doesn't know," said Magnus. "They may be deadly enemies or they may be friendly, though it's hard to imagine anyone being on friendly terms with the Venusians. Actually, the Venusians exist only as a nameless menace to the Bamus. Incidentally, the Bamus are only one of a number of tribes who inhabit this area of Venus. There's always bitter tribal warfare going on, for no particular reason that I can discover. I think it's simply because they like fighting – it provides colour and adventure for them in this pretty drab world. I'm afraid the Bamus are rather a bloodthirsty crowd."

"You were saying about the Venusians?" prompted the Captain.

"The Bamus have never seen them. But all the tribes know of the lake where they live. Some bold tribesmen have, in the distant past, climbed the mountains which surround it and gone down into the bowl, by the lakeside. Some ate the fruit which grows there and reverted to primitive, brainless beasts – like poor Ken did. Others just disappeared mysteriously in the mist. And others were killed by acid gas attacks of the kind we experienced. A few escaped to tell of these things. Now no natives will go within miles of the lake. It's one of the two dreaded places they shun."

"Two places?" queried Bruce.

"Yes. The other is the heart of a great forest on a hill between here and the lake. It's shown on our radar map. That's where the Titans – or Mek Men – live."

They all stared at him. Argen, in the bunk, turned over and groaned in his sleep.

"When we're properly organized here, we'll have to pay them a visit," said Bruce, presently. "Unless, of course, they pay us a visit first."

"That's unlikely," said Magnus. "They seldom leave the forest – so Argen tells me. But you can certainly pay *them* a visit, Baldy – by train. That is, when we get it back on the track."

"Confusion et cetera," said Bruce, amazed. "That railway line goes to the forest?"

"Directly. And the Meks built it, as they built the village pool. You see, they have a working agreement with the Bamus. The Bamus mine the iron ore, load it in the trucks, and drive it to the forest, where they dump it. In return, they're allowed to chop down some of the smaller of the outer trees of the forest and bring them back for building purposes. That was a load we saw. No wonder they looked hastily trimmed – they were. The Bamus are scared stiff of the Meks, and hate to linger near the forest."

"You say the Meks seldom quit the forest. Yet they went to the Moon," said Cliff.

90

"Apparently. But Argen knows nothing of that. I couldn't make him understand about Earth, the Moon and the stars. The Bamus have never seen them, of course, and can't imagine them. Argen thinks we've come from another part of Venus – which, by the way, he doesn't even know is a globe."

"Do I gather the Bamus sweat all day digging with primitive tools for ore in exchange for a few miserable trees?" asked the Captain.

"Things are valuable in relation to their scarcity," replied Magnus. "There's precious few trees in these here parts, except for the Meks' forest. But wood is the least of it. The really rare commodity on Venus, it seems, is water. The water in the pool is piped from the forest – also in exchange for the ore. If the Meks think the Bamus haven't produced enough on any particular day, they cut down the water supply – sometimes cut it off altogether for a period. They have the Bamus by the ears."

'And the Meks have cut the water off now?" asked Bruce.

"They must have done. But why they have we can only guess. Is it because somehow they know the Bamus aren't working, as they should be, at the diggings? Or because they knew we were helping ourselves to the water? We emptied the whole pool in one big suck. Their instruments probably told them that. They knew the Bamus wouldn't – in fact, couldn't – do such a thing. I believe they know we're here, because I believe the Meks fired at our ship when it was about to land. Who else could have done it?"

They agreed it was probably the Meks. And it didn't cheer them to reflect that these giants were hostile to them too. They could be really dangerous enemies. Quite apart from their obvious physical size and strength, they had a formidable technical ability, in some ways superior to that of the Earthmen. It looked as though the human colony on Venus was in for a pretty thin time.

Captain Browne raised another point. "If the Meks need the ore so badly – what do they do with it, I wonder? – why don't they mine it themselves? Or at least provide the Bamus with proper excavating machines, which plainly they could make?"

Magnus shrugged. "It's just another riddle. They don't deal with the Bamus only, you know. All the other tribes around here have to mine for them – various different metals, and coal too, I understand. For the same rewards: timber, water, and a private railway line. All the lines converge on the forest."

"What about the Titan – Mek, rather – who lives in the big

house in the village?" asked Cliff. "Is he the local overseer?"

"No one lives in that house," said Magnus. "It's something between a museum and a temple. All those weapons in it are relics – revered relics, too – the Bamus found at different times when tree-felling on the outskirts of the forest. The Bamus, being fighting mad themselves, believe that the Meks sometimes scrap among themselves, and these were things lost on the battlefield – their owners killed, maybe."

"You've certainly pumped Argen hard," said Bruce. "Did he tell you why he was dumped on us?"

"Yes – a sacrifice, as we guessed. When the rest fled the village, it was he who stayed to wage war on us. One man alone, as I told you. Yes, he's to blame for Lamburn's condition. I've told him about that. I also made him understand that our setting the village on fire was a pure accident, not an act of war. And that afterwards we were trying to save it. So now he's sorry he shot at us and is worried about Lamburn. I told him that if Lamburn dies, then it's the law of the Earthmen that the killer be put to death."

"I say, that's hardly fair," protested Captain Browne. "Argen thought he was fighting a war – "

"I know, I know," interrupted Magnus. "But it gives us a hold over Argen which we may need if we want him to do anything for us."

"Actually, Lamburn's on the mend," said Bruce. "I went to see him this morning."

"Glad to hear it," said Magnus. "But we needn't tell Argen that – yet. As I was saying, when Argen's solitary attack failed, he hared off after the others and found they'd all taken shelter down in the pit. He called them all cowards – Argen's got plenty of guts – and was rallying them for a counter-attack when Cliff and I came ambling down among them."

"And, of course, they saw us coming," said Cliff.

"Yes. They *can* see much farther through the mist than us. Argen promptly split his forces into two to attack us from both sides. But they hadn't reckoned with the 'vibes.' They shook them – literally. Now they regard us with almost as much respect as they regard the Meks. They certainly won't attack us again. They found the wrecked train, and thought we'd done it deliberately to punish them. Then they found the pool empty, and, again, thought the same thing – or at least, that the Meks were punishing them for attacking us. As Argen was the ringleader of the attack, and had already boasted that he'd killed two of us –

an exaggeration – they all rounded on him and used him for a scapegoat. They delivered him to us in an attempt to appease us."

The subject of the discourse at this point sat up, yawned, looked about him, remembered his position, and obviously became a little apprehensive. He looked anxiously at Magnus, as though he were wondering if he were still in the Earthmen's good books. Magnus reassured him with a grin, and Argen rose gingerly from the bunk.

After a glance through his piecemeal dictionary, Magnus spoke to him haltingly. Argen replied briefly.

"What did he say?" asked Bruce.

"He wants some more potatoes. He thinks they're wonderful. Compared with them, Venusian potatoes are apparently – um – small potatoes."

"I think breakfast all round is a good idea," Bruce decided. "Afterwards, we can discuss the next move."

"The next move is obvious," said Magnus. "We'll have to call on the Meks and see if we, too, can fix a deal with them about water. They seem to be running the only local waterworks – apart from the Venusians sitting on *their* supply."

"H'm," murmured Bruce. "They also seem to converse with the aid of spiked clubs and bombshells. I can't say I'm looking forward to that sort of cosy chat. Can't Argen here see them first and sort of pave the way to a friendly introduction?"

"Argen has seen only one of them, and that only once and from a distance," said Magnus. "It seems, like some Indian sects, the Meks feel insulted if anyone of lower caste even dares to look at them. Why, when the battery in the locomotive needs replacing, which is only once in several years, the Bamus have to leave the train overnight at the forest, and return to collect it in the morning. They've never seen the Meks at work. Before the Meks came to install the metal pool in the village, they insisted that all the inhabitants first remove to an area twenty miles away and stay there for a week."

"I don't get that," said Cliff. "How could the Meks 'insist' if the Bamus never see them? I mean, how do the Meks make their wishes known?"

Magnus answered slowly: "They use thought-rods – exactly similar to the one the Venusians sent to us."

There was such a loud chorus of exclamation that Argen took a step back, startled.

Then Bruce said: "You're an awkward cuss, Magnus. I thought

you were explaining and clearing things up so nicely. And then you go and drop a bomb like that."

"Some day," said Magnus, "I hope to be able to explain that part of the puzzle also. But at the moment I haven't a clue. Did someone suggest breakfast?"

"'Tato?" asked Argen, plaintively.

"Much 'tato," said Magnus, patting his shoulder. "Plenty munch."

CHAPTER SEVEN

THE MEK FOREST

The would-be colonists in *Archimedes II* were becoming restless. They had been confined to the ship for a long time. It seemed ages to them since they left the Moon. And now, at last on Venus, they were still confined to the ship. They were men picked for their energy and enthusiasm, and naturally they fretted at this inactivity.

They didn't complain, but Bruce sensed the feeling. At breakfast he told the others he was worried about it.

Magnus seemed rudely to ignore him and held a quiet conversation with Argen. Apparently, he found it difficult to capture Argen's attention, for the pale savage was watching with fascination the others' skill with knives and forks. He didn't attempt to ape them, but slid segments of fried potato into his mouth with his fingers.

However, Magnus got the information he wanted. Then he said: "Don't worry, Baldy. Give them a pep talk over the blower, and tell 'em there's a good chance they'll be able to go out for a walk and some air today. Argen's going to tell the village folk that we're on their side, and it's safe for them to return home. Also, we'll put the train back on the rails for them, and get the pool functioning again – so long as they'll promise to give up trying to make pin-cushions out of us."

"You seem recklessly generous with your promises," said Bruce.

"It'll work out," said Magnus, carelessly. "You'll see."

As an indication of the respect Bruce held for Magnus's judgment, ten minutes later he was cheerfully informing all and sundry over the loudspeaker system that soon they would be let loose on Venus.

Presently the gangplank was lowered, but solely for Argen, who staggered down it under the weight of a sack of raw potatoes. He was going to distribute samples of this luscious food the Earthmen had brought. Also to tell his people that the Earthmen intended to grow potatoes here in great numbers, not only for themselves, but for the Bamus also.

looks feasible. But I'm darned if I'm going to amble up to them saying 'How do you do?' and holding my hand out – and then just get clubbed in return."

"That's a fine idea!" said Cliff, enthusiastically.

"What – me getting clubbed?"

"No – camouflaging ourselves as chunks of mineral."

"I didn't say ourselves. I said me. Don't say you want to come, too?"

"No," said Cliff. "I shan't say that – it wouldn't be true. I'm not a born hero, but I'd hoped to become one, with experience. But now I've given up even that hope. I seem to get scared of things more and more as time goes on. But we *are* partners, and if ever I get scared enough to forget that, then that will be the day I resign from the S.I.D."

Magnus's lean face creased in a grin.

"Have a cigar," he said, producing his case. "And three rousing cheers for the S.I.D., confound it. We all get scared, Cliff – even old Baldy. And now we'd better go and look for him, and see what he thinks of our plan."

They found Beckworth Bruce in the village square, a slight, shrivelled figure gazing pensively at the empty metal pool.

Nearby, a couple of technicians were fiddling with a box, replete with dials and knobs, fastened to the chest of a third. The third man wore earphones and an anxious expression. It was obvious that if he were hearing anything at all, it wasn't what it should be. He was holding a metal plate, at the end of a stick, a few inches above the ground.

"Trouble, Baldy?" asked Magnus, his voice breaking into one of its unexpected squeaks.

"A gremlin in the works," said Bruce. "These confounded electronic detectors are always going on the blink. We were doing fine, too. The pool is supplied by a metal pipe, about a yard underground, I'd say. The detector picked it up clearly. We followed it for about a hundred yards and then the detector packed up."

"Along that street, of course," said Magnus, flicking a thumb at it.

Bruce nodded.

"I thought so," said Magnus. "That's the line, as the crow flies, to the Mek forest. I don't think you'll find the blockage anywhere around Lomba, old man. It's more likely to be at the Meks' end."

While he was talking, Magnus was peering between the technicians into the detector box. Then he reached in and gave something half a turn.

The wearer of the apparatus smiled suddenly and gave a thumbs up sign. He was hearing the proper signal.

"I thought so," said Magnus. "That little plug is always coming loose. It needs a clip."

Not for the first time Cliff realized he would never, in all his career, make half such a good all-round S.I.D. man as Martin Magnus. Trouble-shooting in any sphere came as naturally as breathing to Magnus.

"I'd rather dig here than at the other end," remarked Bruce.

"Please yourself," said Magnus easily. "But I'll be going along to the other end later today, so if I can save you any trouble by asking the Meks to look into it, I'll be happy to oblige."

Bruce gave him one of his hard, keen stares.

"All right, Magnus, I can see you've cooked up something. What is it?"

Magnus explained his plan. Bruce was persuaded, after some argument, but added: "Bear this in mind, though, the pair of you: you're going merely to spy out the land. Don't try to tangle with the Meks: you can't afford to give all that weight away. Keep out of sight. And hurry back. Incidentally, you'll have to leave it till tomorrow."

"Why?" asked Magnus.

Bruce tapped his watch. "We're no longer on the twenty-four hour clock – remember? We've used up the whole morning getting the train back on the rails. The Bamus won't have time now before dark to dig out enough ore to make a full load. And it had better be a full load, or the Meks might start asking questions in some unpleasant way or another."

"Oh, that's all right," said Magnus. "I'll take care of that with the half-tracks and a couple of reels of blasting tape."

Bruce opened his eyes a bit wider.

"You think of everything," he said, almost grudgingly.

"But they'll hear the B.T. in the Mek forest," said Cliff, frowning. "The Meks will wonder what the dickens we're up to."

"Let 'em," said Magnus. "We've done our share of wondering what the dickens *they're* up to, so it'll be quits."

He and Cliff went back to the ship to collect the blasting tape. They rounded up the two half-track drivers, and then in procession, taking the trailers also, they drove alongside the railway track towards the mineral diggings. The train had already departed for the same destination. They encountered a few lanky,

99

mop-headed Bamus plodding along in that direction, but they saw nothing of Argen. Presumably, he had gone on ahead in the train, with the bulk of the natives.

When they came to the downward slope, the half-tracks negotiated it cautiously, winding between the deeper diggings and crunching across the shallower ones that couldn't be avoided. Presently, they came to the diggers themselves, plying with spades and picks as though their lives depended upon it – as perhaps they did, for they had no water beyond what remained in the clay vessels in their shacks.

Magnus pointed up the slope to the left. Following his indication, Cliff could just discern the ghostly outline of the train standing motionless at the crest of the long slope. Picking their slow way up to it was a string of Bamus. Each carried on his shoulders a twig-basket full of ore. The baskets weren't large, but plainly they held as heavy a load as these rather frail people could manage.

Magnus commented: "Bruce was right. They'll never fill the trucks today at that rate."

They continued on and came across Argen attacking a large lump of crude ore with a pick, breaking it up into more manageable pieces. He paused to give them a welcoming grin and mop his forehead with the back of his thin hand. Magnus jumped down to speak to him, and in a few minutes the word was going round among the Bamus that the Earthmen had come to help them in their labours.

They came dancing excitedly around the half-tracks. But they looked rather doubtful when Magnus told them they were all – every one of them – to go to the far side of the train and wait there until further orders. Nevertheless, they trooped obediently up the slope. Argen wished to stay, but Magnus made him go too.

Then Magnus and Cliff, assisted by the two drivers after they had removed their vehicles to a safe distance, began to lay out the blasting tape.

This stuff was as light and thin as magnesium in strip form. It was about an inch wide and comfortably flexible: a lot of it could be wound on to one reel. Indeed, it looked just like magnesium on one side. The other side was jet black.

It was a synthetic metal produced after a long process in an atomic reaction plant, and it had a chemical name almost as long as the process. It was popularly called "B.T." – short for "blasting tape."

A lot of power had gone into arranging the molecular structure

100

of its brighter side, which was not a stable one, and much of that same power would be released suddenly if the molecular structure were now disturbed. But not even an atomic explosion could disintegrate the black surface, which acted as a kind of mirror to the explosive energy, reflecting it back along its own path or at an angle of incidence.

The four Earthmen laid out two whole reels of the tape, black face uppermost, thirty yards apart along the ground, right across the diggings, far down the slope. Then they joined the wondering Bamus behind the train, well away from the nearer ends of the B.T. Magnus was holding a thin case – it was no bigger than his cigar case. He opened it, looked at the row of gleaming transistors, made a slight adjustment, and snapped the case shut again. He knelt and laid it on the ground before him.

Argen, who was standing nearby, eyed it suspiciously and began to edge away. The other natives, taking their cue from him, began to do the same.

Magnus stopped them with a single word of command. Aside, he said to Cliff and the drivers: "Lie down and cover your ears."

They lay down and clapped their hands tightly over their ears.

Magnus said something to Argen, who repeated it with some embellishment to the crowd. They all flopped to the ground and covered their ears. Some, perhaps to show their enthusiasm but more probably because of fright, also closed their eyes.

With a last look round at them, Magnus moved three sliding knobs – all very tiny – on the upper face of the little case. It was a radio transmitter, and now it began to transmit – on three different wavelengths. These would modulate and change until two of them cancelled themselves out and the third, the vital one, would send its unimpeded call at growing strength to the precariously balanced molecules in the B.T.

It was a complicated but necessary programme, and it took five seconds to complete – just time enough for Magnus to settle himself also at full length on the ground, ears blocked.

It was hardly worth the trouble of settling himself comfortably, for almost at once there came a terrific shock. It hit them all, through the ground, as though Mek Men were buried alive there and were hammering with giant fists to get out.

In the next instant, a tremendous clap of sound leaped up from the slope beyond and below the railway track. There came a rushing wind, driving the mist before it and compressing it into a dark cloud-ball which rolled over them. For a minute it seemed that night had come before its time.

101

Then the cloud passed, leaving in its wake clearer air than they'd ever seen on Venus.

Cliff got to his knees, and saw Magnus doing the same. His senses were swimming.

The Bamus were still all lying around, most of them with their faces buried in their arms. Argen lay with his mouth wide open. Cliff fancied he was yelling with surprise, or fright, or both. But he couldn't hear him, for a thousand bells seemed to be ringing in his ears.

Magnus stood up and began shouting also, but it was some time before Cliff could hear anything of him. He was repeating some Bamu words over and over, and Cliff guessed he was trying to reassure the natives. But it was to little or no effect. As soon as they were able to stand, most of the villagers fled. Cliff was glad to see Argen was not among them. So was Magnus. He went over and gave Argen a comradely pat on the back. The native looked even more white-faced than usual, but he stood his ground, and managed a sort of scared grin at Magnus.

All was quiet again now, and the mist was returning.

"I always said Argen had more guts than the rest of them," said Magnus, giving the man a final pat. "Gosh, Cliff, I overdid that, didn't I! One strip – no, half a strip – would have been plenty. B.T. certainly packs a punch. Are you all right, Mark? How about you, Jim?"

These last questions were addressed to the drivers. They each affirmed that they were still roughly in one piece, though Mark complained of a headache and Jim of deafness.

"Time will heal – you'll be okay in a few minutes," promised Magnus. "Now let's inspect the damage. Thank heavens the train stayed on the track. For one horrible moment I was afraid it was coming off again."

They walked round it and looked down the far slope. From this distance they could see only the beginning of the two enormous parallel furrows in the ground, dug out by the fury of the B.T. flinging its might downwards.

With Argen in their midst, the four of them walked down the narrow track between the huge, but perfectly straight, furrows. The iron ore had been torn wholesale from the earth and lay in endless heaps.

"Look at it," said Magnus, digging Argen with his elbow. "All just waiting there for you to pick up."

He spoke in English but Argen gathered his meaning, grinned

102

again, and shouted something over his shoulder to the handful of following villagers.

"Do you think you can get your trucks along here, boys?" Magnus asked Mark and Jim.

They thought it would be easy.

"Right," said Magnus. "Take them round to the bottom and bring them up this track when I signal. I'll tell Argen to collect the flock together again, and then we'll get organized."

Soon, Magnus's plan was working smoothly. Along the inner lip of each furrow a long line of natives stood, the raw ore heaped around them, their shovels and baskets ready. Up the narrow track between them came lumbering slowly first one half-track, with its trailer, then the other. From both sides the natives emptied their baskets into them as they passed, and then flung more than one shovelful of loose pieces in afterwards.

The vehicles arrived at the top end of the furrows fully loaded, and ground up and on to the train, where another waiting team boarded them and shovelled the ore from them into the open trucks as the vehicles moved slowly along parallel to the line.

Then Mark and Jim would drive rapidly down the slope, skirting the furrows, and turn to repeat the conveyor-belt process.

There would be no trouble about unloading the train at the Mek forest, for, as had been discovered during the morning's work, each truck was of the tip-up kind, actuated by one of the now familiar buttons set in its forepart. Argen, of course, already knew about that, but hadn't thought it worth mentioning. Surely, he asked, when reproached, the Earthmen knew all there was to know about machines?

Surprisingly quickly, the task was ended. The train was fully loaded, save for the truck immediately behind the engine. A cunning space had been left here to accommodate Magnus and Cliff, so that they could lie in it, largely hidden. They hadn't told Argen what this was for, but manifestly he was concerned about it and kept eyeing them questioningly.

At length, he asked Magnus openly.

Magnus, who was examining the dial of his "vibe," hooked the weapon back on to its sling. He answered in Bamu. Cliff watched the dismay spread over Argen's face. Magnus argued quietly with him, until Argen went silent and would not answer.

"I gather the verdict isn't favourable," Cliff commented.

"It's not. It seems that no one likes taking the train to the forest at any time. They really dread the place. They have a roster – a different driver each day, for there's nothing to driving the thing: a child could do it. The fellow supposed to be on duty today hopped off into the mist when we let the big cracker off. He hasn't come back, and no one feels like taking his place. However, Argen says he'll go, if it means Lomba will get its water supply again. But he's scared of the consequences if we go with him and get caught spying on the Meks. In that case, he's sure of two things. We shall get it in the neck, 'vibes' or no 'vibes.' And Lomba will not only be deprived of water for good – the Meks will trample it into the earth."

"He may be right, at that," said Cliff.

"Yes, I see his point of view. We'll just have to go without him."

"But if the Meks see one of us driving the train, instead of the customary Bamu, they'll start reaching for their triggers – or bow-strings."

"Can't be helped, Cliff. We'll have to risk that."

"We've still got one card up our sleeves. Remember, we've told Argen his life depends on whether Lamburn lives or dies. We know Lamburn is out of danger now – but Argen doesn't. We could bargain with him – offer him clemency in return for his doing this job."

Magnus gave Cliff a quizzical look. "Trying to hoist me with my own petard, eh? When I thought of using that yarn as a big stick, I didn't know Argen well enough. We've learned since that he has loyalty and integrity and a sense of civic duty, besides courage. Lies and threats are poor weapons against a man of his character. What respect would he have for Earthman's justice if he learned he could dodge its penalties by doing something he didn't believe was right?"

Cliff didn't answer. Magnus beckoned Mark and Jim. They came over.

Magnus said: "You two had better get back to Bruce now – you can give some of this mob a lift. Tell him Cliff and I are taking the excursion train to the forest."

As the half-tracks drove off, laden with boisterous natives enjoying the novelty of the ride, Magnus told Argen to return to Lomba also, taking with him the remainder of the villagers.

Argen answered in his own tongue: "I cannot go. I must deliver this load of ore."

"Then tell them to go, and remain here," Magnus said, in Bamu.

When the last of the natives had disappeared into the mist, village-bound, Magnus told the forlorn Argen: "We are deliver-

104

ing this load. You may come with us if you like. If not, you can stay here till we return. That is up to you. We are not afraid of the Meks. We are stronger than they. We shall make them give Lomba water again. Now, what do you say?"

Argen shuffled his feet in the stress of indecision.

Finally, he made an answer, and climbed slowly into the driving cockpit of the locomotive. Magnus winked covertly at Cliff. They heaved themselves into the truck behind and settled into the prepared hollow. Then the train began to carry them off towards the unknown.

As it rolled along, Cliff asked Magnus: "What made him decide to take us, after all?"

"He said that the Earthmen had not lied to him so far, and therefore he would believe us when we said we were stronger than the Meks and would make them open up the waterworks again. So now we've got to live up to our boast. We can't lie to him now, can we?"

Cliff made no comment, but began to check his "vibe."

Magnus watched him, and smiled to himself. Privately, he thought "vibes" of this limited capacity were unlikely to halt a raging giant. They would have to use cunning rather than force.

On they went, mile after mile. They could see little of the landscape, but it seemed to be becoming more uneven than around Lomba. Twice they had glimpses of deep ravines. Presently they could see even less, for the mist appeared to be thickening. The train was travelling more slowly.

"We're climbing," said Magnus. "Gradually – but steadily."

Now and then they perceived the shapes of bushes with heavy, broad leaves, and then isolated saplings. Then came a whole grove of young trees, and patches of stumps where the Bamus had been felling.

"We must be nearly there," said Cliff, his mouth a little dry.

They arrived quite suddenly at the real edge of the forest. Enormous trees, like the redwoods of the Amazonian forests (although they could estimate their height only from the thickness of their boles), stood close-packed on either side of them, giant palisades.

The train went on for some distance into the forest, then stopped.

The pair stood up, wonderingly. There seemed small danger of their being seen, because they could see so little themselves – though it did cross Cliff's mind that, as the Bamus could see so much better than they, then it was likely the Meks could also.

They were in a wide, gloomy avenue. The mist pressed down, like a solid ceiling scarce twenty feet above their heads, cutting sharply across the boles of the trees so that they looked like a row of great stumps.

The same thin grass carpeted the hard ground between them.

It was as silent as a cathedral at night – and as eerie.

Along one side of the railway line was an irregular layer of rough, rocky lumps – the residue of the last load of iron ore which had been dumped here. The line itself ran on down the avenue into darkness. Magnus pointed along it and looked inquiringly at Argen. Argen, climbing down from the locomotive, made the peculiar bob of the head which, in the language of Bamu gestures, meant a decisive "No." He indicated the dumping ground, muttering.

"He says no Bamus are allowed to go beyond this point," Magnus translated. "They must dump their ore here and leave at once."

"Ask him where he saw the Mek Man," prompted Cliff.

Magnus did so. Argen pointed down the avenue, towards the heart of the forest, and amplified his meaning with speech.

"He didn't depart immediately one day, and saw the Mek coming, presumably to inspect the load," reported Magnus. "And then he *did* depart – in a hurry. Now he's anxious to get shot of this load too, and get off the mark. We'd better give him a hand."

Argen was already moving back along the train, stopping to press the button which tipped each truck as he passed. They caught him up and went on ahead, until the whole load had been deposited in one long mound at the side of the track. Then they worked their way back to the engine, righting each truck as they came to it.

Magnus had a short conversation with Argen. The emaciated native, showing up palely white against the murky background and looking like some wild, ghostly spirit of the woods, climbed unhappily back into the driving cockpit. Then all at once he reached out to shake each of them by the hand – an Earth custom he had learned and suddenly remembered.

Then he settled in and began to back the train along the avenue, back towards the entrance to the woods. Very soon he was out of sight, and they were alone in the giants' forest.

Cliff was getting the too familiar feeling of having butterflies in his stomach. Perhaps Magnus had it too, but if so it didn't show. He said, cheerfully: "Argen's going to wait for us,

106

with the train, a mile or so back, where the bushes are. He's promised to wait until it's almost dark."

"That won't be very long now," said Cliff, not cheerfully. "I hate these short days."

"It's no worse than winter in England," said Magnus. "We've still a couple of hours left for exploring. I suggest we follow the railway line a bit farther."

"All right, but not too far, if we've got to walk all that way back to the train."

He fell in beside Magnus. They walked on, deeper into the forest, looking about them. Nothing stirred. There seemed to be no animal, bird or insect life, and no flowers or small plants. Just the dead straight rails, the grass, the thick bases of the trees, and the mist all around and above.

"I'd hate to get lost in here," said Cliff. "The Babes in the Wood was never one of my favourite stories. Come to think of it" – he shivered slightly – "neither was Jack the Giant-killer."

Magnus gripped his arm and halted him. Wordlessly, he pointed to the ground just ahead of them. It was a softer patch than the rest, and startlingly clearly in it was set a deep impression: the footprint of a giant, its toe towards them. And Cliff shivered again.

He tried to say something, and achieved only a gulp. The gloom and hidden threat of these grotesque woods had been playing subtly on his nerves.

Magnus knelt and studied the print. "Six inches deep and about six feet long. What size in boots is that?"

But Cliff was still dumb.

"Definitely a boot," Magnus said, half to himself. "I reckon that makes him around forty feet tall. Maybe a bit more. With a stride of six or seven yards – yes, look, you can just see the print of the other foot yonder. But it's harder ground there and doesn't show the impression anything like so well. I expect we've passed several without noticing 'em."

"I wonder," croaked Cliff, recovering something of his voice, "how many of *those* we've passed without noticing 'em?"

He was pointing to a tree on the far side of the avenue.

"Good heavens!" Magnus looked hard at it.

Deeply embedded in the trunk was a huge arrow, just like the ones they'd seen in Linné and the big house in Lomba.

They crossed the line and went over for a closer look and soon discovered half a dozen other arrows sticking in the trees round

107

about. Magnus wrenched at some of them but failed to remove any.

"They've gone in with the force of a rocket," he said. "It just shows what those bows can do if you *are* able to bend 'em."

"Archery practice?" suggested Cliff.

"Perhaps. Only, these particular arrows must have fallen short of the target, which surely must be on their eye-level – up there in the mist."

Cliff was smitten by a not too happy thought. "Yes, of course – any Mek Man walking around at this altitude must literally be walking with his head in the clouds. So, like the Bamus, their eyes must be accustomed to the mist."

"Yes, it places us at a further disadvantage, doesn't it?" said Magnus. "Compared with them, we're not only tiny creatures but also half-blind ones."

Cliff looked at his watch. "Don't you think we ought to be starting back soon?" He tried not to sound too eager.

"Not just yet," said Magnus. "Darn it, we've not seen a Mek yet. We can't leave until we have – else what's the point of coming here at all? There's a good chance that one or two will be coming along soon to give the latest load of ore the once-over and check that the Bamus haven't tried to short-change them. I expect the one Argen saw was coming to do that. Let's go back to the dump and wait there."

"All right," said Cliff, resignedly. At least, the dump was nearer to the outskirts of the forest.

They struck out obliquely back towards the avenue, rounded a particularly thick tree and all but walked into an enormous pyramidal helmet, of recognizable design, lying just beyond it. Beside it lay a great sword, its blade snapped clean off not far from the hilt.

Magnus whistled, and then spotted something gleaming dully in the grass a few yards to one side. He went over and picked it up. It was the other part of the broken sword-blade, narrowing to a disturbingly acute point. Cliff glanced at it briefly, then turned to feel a long, deep dent in the helmet.

"Look at this, Magnus."

Magnus whistled again and came to examine it.

"Tweedledum and Tweedledee agreed to have a battle," he murmured. "It looks as though the Bamus were right – the Meks are quarrelsome gentry. Whoever owned this tin hat got the worst of it this time. Do you see any somewhat bulky corpses lying around?"

108

"No, and I don't want to," said Cliff, emphatically. "Let's get back to the avenue. I feel happier there – if not much."

Magnus threw down the pieces of sword-blade.

"If the Bamus want these things for their museum, they can darn well come and carry 'em," he said.

Back in the avenue, they walked quickly along to the ore dump. Magnus glanced at it cursorily. "It doesn't appear to have been touched," he said, and was about to turn away when he noticed something half-buried under the rocky lumps. He dragged it out. It was one of the wire cables they had used that morning when righting the train. Someone had left it, coiled neatly, in the bottom of a truck. It had been tipped out here together with the ore which had been loaded on top of it.

He was regarding it thoughtfully when a tiny lump of ore, perched on the top of the heap, suddenly rolled to the bottom. Yet nothing visible had touched it.

Then another, larger, lump followed it and started a miniature avalanche down the side of the heap.

"What's doing that?" asked Cliff, curiously.

Magnus raised a forefinger to his lips. They stood perfectly still, listening. And became aware of a distant, slow and deliberate thumping sound. At each faint thump, another trickle of rock dust and small lumps meandered down the dump.

"It's like the hammer of Thor," whispered Magnus. "Are they working in the smithy?"

"They're getting louder," said Cliff, huskily. And then the cold thrill of realization shot through him. "They're getting nearer. They're *footsteps*!"

"Behind that tree!" said Magnus, urgently, and they scuttled around one of the biggest trees in the avenue. The roots were high and far spreading. They crouched down between two of them. Cliff kept his head well down, but Magnus kept peeping over the top.

Soon they themselves were feeling the ground tremors which had shaken down the small rock fragments. The impacts became heavier and heavier. And nearer and nearer.

Thump ... Thump ... Thump ...

In time to them, Magnus began to hum softly the Anvil Chorus from *Il Trovatore*.

Then: "I can see him!" he breathed, suddenly, excitedly. "Look!"

Cliff was quite sure he didn't want to look, but all the same he did.

Emerging from the shadows and mist down the avenue was a huge pair of legs, walking slowly towards them. Thick as ordinary tree trunks, they were, but otherwise quite human-seeming. From the knees down they were encased in what appeared to be steel gaiters, or armour, with flaps reaching almost to the toes of the great black boots. Above the knees, the bulging thighs were covered with some tight-fitting dark material, and dissolved into the low ceiling of mist.

Ponderously, they marched down the avenue, the ground quivering like a drum-skin at every step. Regularly, too, there came the sound of air being breathed in and expelled.

Even in the face of this, Magnus had to joke. In a moment between the thudding steps, he whispered in Cliff's ear: "He's asthmatic!"

But Cliff was scarcely in the frame of mind to appreciate humour. He crouched down between the roots, saying silent prayers.

The massive tread stopped just at the other side of their tree. Nothing but the heavy breathing sound could be heard. They guessed the Mek was making a tally of the ore. Unless, of course, his keener eyes had seen them . . .

After an age of screaming suspense, the heart-shaking footsteps began again, going away from them.

Cautiously, Magnus peered round the bole, after them.

"He's still going on," he reported. "Towards the edge of the forest – the way we came in. Gosh, I hope he doesn't spot the train waiting out there!"

Cliff dared to look too, just in time to see a back view of the giant's legs walking into the mist.

"What do we do now?" he asked, and was ashamed because his voice was trembling.

"We wait for him to come back," said Magnus, firmly. "I'm curious to learn how they shift this ore. Perhaps this gentleman scoops it up in a bag and carries it off – though that would mean plenty of trips, even for him."

He paused, and looked again at the cable he was still holding.

"Trips," he repeated, softly. "That's an idea."

"What is?"

"Half a giant may be better than no giant," said Magnus, "but it's rather frustrating. I want to see what a whole Mek looks like. We must bring him down to our level."

He began uncoiling the thin, but very strong, cable.

110

"Now what?" asked Cliff, in lively alarm, half guessing the answer.

"We trip him up as he comes back," said Magnus. Which was the answer Cliff had anticipated and dreaded.

The now distant thumps stopped suddenly.

"He'll be turning back any moment," snapped Magnus. "Come on, give me a hand."

From Magnus's expression Cliff saw that his mind was made up and argument would be futile. If he wouldn't help, Magnus would attempt it alone. So Cliff took the proffered end of the cable and ran round the tree with it, meeting Magnus coming the opposite way at the other side.

They tied a non-slip knot, and ran the rest of the cable across the avenue to an almost equally stout tree on the far side. There was little cable to spare to tie it there, but somehow, with the extra energy of desperation, they knotted that end securely also. The cable was stretched nearly taut, a yard or so above the ground.

As they hurried back to their hiding place between the roots, the gargantuan footsteps could be heard – and felt – returning.

Cliff lay low beside Magnus, the sweat pouring from him.

Would the Mek see the snare? Would it be shriekingly obvious to his keener eyesight? But the cable was quite thin, and the dusk was starting to gather in the already shadowy wood. There was a chance it might work.

And then Cliff found himself fighting down a disgraceful little hope growing in his mind that not only would the Mek not notice the cable, but also step clean over it, and pass on, oblivious to it and to them, back to his mysterious dwelling in the forest.

Thump . . . Thump . . . Thump . . .

Cliff's mind began to freeze up altogether now. He just lay, waiting, while the shudders of a minor earthquake seemed to spread right through the dark forest. The steps were almost beside them.

Then: *Twang!* The cable snapped and whipped back.

They both started and sat up. Fascinated and wide-eyed, they saw the monstrous legs stumbling, then falling forwards.

The giant's waist became visible, and then they both cried aloud in surprise and horror at what they saw.

Or rather – at what they didn't see.

111

CHAPTER EIGHT

THE SECRET OF THE MEKS

For above the waist the giant didn't exist!

He ended at a metal chain waist-belt as neatly as if he had been sliced in two like a carrot. Tumbling head-first from the top of the trousers, as though just emptied from them, was what appeared – to the startled watchers – to be a small boy.

His legs were miniature replicas of those he was falling from, even to the steel gaiters. He was wearing a similar waist-belt too. But the rest of him was unmistakably there, in a black tunic. His arms were stretched out before him in an attempt to break his fall. His peaked little face was as white as a Bamu's, but his thick mop of hair was dark – as dark as his wide, horrified eyes.

He did break his fall to some extent, but not enough. It had been a long drop, and his head hit the hard ground with a thwack. The frightened eyes closed in unconsciousness.

The huge, disembodied legs had rolled sideways and lay there, still marching but getting nowhere – they were only flailing the empty air. The effect was both ridiculous and bizarre, especially as the heavy panting went on.

Magnus bounded out into the avenue. He glanced down at the small, motionless figure, but didn't stop. He leaped to the waist of the great legs and fumbled around there. Before Cliff was properly to his feet, the fantastic legs slowed in mid-kick and stopped with a sigh.

But Cliff was more concerned about the little fellow than them. He turned him over carefully and lifted and cradled his head. He pushed the thick hair back from the forehead and saw the bruise gathering there. It was not a boy's face, though the figure was only three feet tall and boyish-seeming. It was a pale, lined little face, rather elfin.

Magnus came back and stood over them.

"Is he all right?"

"He's still breathing," said Cliff. "I was afraid he'd broken his neck."

"You mean, that *I'd* broken his neck," said Magnus, soberly. "But then, in my wildest dreams I never imagined a set-up like this. I thought we were tackling a giant – not a little chap dressed up in an enormous wolf's clothing. Those legs – they look amazingly realistic, but they're only mechanical. There's a little driving seat set inside the waist, with the usual three-button control. That's where he tumbled from. He gave his head a shocking bang. Looks like he'll be out for some time. Wish we had some water."

"I could do with a drink myself," said Cliff, licking his lips and looking round the darkling forest. "We'll have to get back. Argen won't wait much longer for us. Shall we leave this little chap here?"

"Not likely!" said Magnus. "We wanted to meet a Mek Man, didn't we? Well, here's one – cut down to his proper size. We'll appoint him the official representative of the Meks and take him home for a chat – and some medical attention. I'll be happier when the Doc's given him a check-up."

He bent down and lifted the limp Mek in his arms.

"We'll take turns at carrying him," he said, and began walking. Cliff delayed a minute to have a quick, close look at the mechanical legs, then hurried after Magnus.

"Did you notice the air vents, just above the hips?" he asked, catching up. "They must be the origin of the noise that sounded like the giant breathing."

"No doubt they were meant to foster that illusion," said Magnus, striding on. "But they're also part of the mechanism. Obviously, it's pneumatic. The legs weren't meant just to walk, but also to stamp – to leave impressions and sound like the tread of a particularly meaty Cyclops. They must contain pneumatic pile-drivers."

"But what's the idea of it all?"

"Surely that's clear enough, Cliff? To frighten all the native tribes which surround the forest away from the idea of ever exploring it. The Meks are little folk, really, trying to kid everyone they're ferocious giants. It all fits in, don't you see? The outsize weapons left lying around, deliberately, to be found by the natives. The stove-in helmet and the broken sword, and the arrows in the trees – no doubt hammered in, probably pneumatically too. All mock-up jobs, all fake. No wonder the Meks, on the rare occasions when they do venture from the forest, always make sure the natives never see 'em!"

Cliff thought about it, then said: "Yes, I suppose that's it. But why did they carry out the same bluff at Linné? There weren't any natives, or any living creatures, there."

Magnus shook his head. "Maybe this little man will tell us, in due course."

"It all seems so unnecessary to me. Compared even with the stringy Bamus, the Meks are puny, physically. That's supposing they are all like this specimen, of course. But they're far from puny technically. What about that gun they fired at the ship? If they can build weapons as powerful as that, then why do they play this childish game with only make-believe weapons?"

"Why?" echoed Magnus.

"They could lord it over the Bamus any time they liked. What does their size matter if they can build guns and trains and, presumably, aeroplanes – if not tanks? Why, they must have built a spaceship to reach the Moon. It was some spaceship, too – remember the size of the lunar base?"

"Yes," said Magnus, briefly. He stumbled.

"My turn," said Cliff, reaching for the still unconscious Mek.

Magnus seemed relieved to hand over the small burden. It was so uncharacteristic that Cliff looked curiously at him. But it was becoming difficult to see clearly even things close to. Night was falling steadily.

"Gosh, I'm tired!" said Magnus. That explained it, of course. Magnus had not slept since *Archimedes II* landed on Venus. He had gone on doing strenuous work without once slackening. But even his prodigious vitality had a limit, and it was reaching it now.

They walked on, feeling every now and again with their feet for the railway lines, checking that they were still on the right track.

Presently, they could see a bit better, for they were leaving the big trees behind, emerging from the forest proper. Nevertheless, the light continued to fail as the short Venusian day departed and the starless, mist-bound night came on. Cliff's arms were aching, but he hadn't the heart to pile the load back on to Magnus.

The Mek was still breathing gently, but had not regained consciousness. Cliff was beginning to worry about him. He didn't want him to die on them.

He kept straining his eyes, searching the gloom ahead for a sign of Argen and the train. He was worrying about that, too. It was near enough night now, and Argen hadn't promised to wait after dark. He couldn't reasonably be expected to.

Magnus walked slowly and silently at his side, swaying a bit now and then. He was all but walking in his sleep.

114

And then the front of the locomotive loomed suddenly in front of them, a mere blur. Magnus leant against the engine, utterly spent. Cliff called: "Argen!"

But there was no answer.

Cliff put the Mek down gently and looked into the driving cockpit. It was empty. He gazed around anxiously, but the dark mist hid everything. He called again. Still there was silence.

"I think Argen's gone home, Magnus," he said.

"No," said Magnus, drowsily. "Argen wouldn't have run away. Maybe he's been spirited away."

"By whom?"

"Who knows?" said Magnus, yawning. "Other Meks, perhaps. Or the Venusians."

That didn't cheer Cliff at all. He said: "We can't very well hang around here. The other Meks may have discovered by now we've kidnapped this chap. They'll be after us – perhaps with that gun . . ."

"Phooey!" said Magnus. "They're scared to come out. I doubt if they'd shoot, anyway, while we've got a hostage. They won't risk killing him too."

"Perhaps they don't care," said Cliff. "But I'm not so scared of them. It's the Venusians. They're really behind them, somehow – I feel it. And they're a sight more dangerous."

"Fish!" said Magnus, tiredly scornful. "They can't get out of their old lake."

"Oh, no – they only came to Earth once," said Cliff, unwontedly sarcastic. "Look, Magnus, you've got twenty trucks to choose from. If you can manage to climb in one, I'll hand the manikin in to you. Keep a hold on him, though. Don't go to sleep, for heaven's sake. Then I'll drive the train back."

"Okay," said Magnus. "I'll leave it to you. Only, don't pile her up at the other end, like I did. Remember, there are no signals on this line."

"I'll watch out," promised Cliff, knowing he was talking nonsense, for it was already impossible to see beyond the first two trucks.

With an obvious effort, Magnus hauled himself into the first truck, the one they had come in. Almost immediately, he exclaimed: "What the – ?"

"What is it?" asked Cliff, in sudden panic.

"Only Argen. I trod on him. He's lying in here asleep." Magnus gave a short laugh. "He was up all last night, too, of course."

"Thank goodness we've found him," said Cliff.

"Wake up, there," said Magnus, prodding away. "Sleeping on duty – you ought to be shot, you old war-horse!"

Argen sat up, rubbing his eyes. Magnus crouched beside him and spoke to him rapidly in Bamu. Argen replied briefly, and climbed out of the truck. He rubbed his eyes again when he saw the Mek lying there, very still on the ground. He looked inquiringly back at Magnus, who said something carelessly and added to Cliff: "Hand up the little man, and get in here yourself. Argen will drive us home. He knows this line with his eyes shut, and he can see better that way than you can with yours open.

Cliff obeyed, relieved. And in a couple of minutes the train was sliding smoothly back along the rails, through the night. Cliff and Magnus lay on the floor of the truck, the Mek between them.

Magnus said, through yawns: "Don't let Argen or any of his tribe learn that this is a real Mek or the Bamus will get so mad at having been fooled by the little men that they'll likely go charging of into the forest to hunt 'em like rabbits. They're spear-happy, you know. We don't want a Bamu-Mek war on our hands to add to our troubles."

"Right," said Cliff.

The train was going at a fair speed now, and Cliff was wondering how far Argen really could see where they were going. He recalled that Argen had once seen what he thought was a Mek Man in the forest. But the fake giant extended only to a short distance above the mist ceiling. Why, then, hadn't the keen-eyed Argen spotted it for what it was, right away?

He asked the question aloud. But the only reply from Magnus was a snore. Cliff smiled quietly to himself and gripped the small wrist of the Mek tighter. Magnus was going to be of little help if the Mek should suddenly regain his senses and try to escape.

So he had to answer the question himself. Argen had seen the giant legs only in the far distance and hadn't paused to take a good look at them. He'd promptly turned and flown for his life.

Cliff's thoughts wandered a good deal after that, and he was near dozing himself when suddenly he became aware of a growing light. He got to his knees, peering over the top of the truck. There, in the direction they were going, was a pair of bright lights shining back at them along the track. He rubbed his eyes. Despite Magnus's jest, *were* there signals on this line?

Then he laughed at himself for a fool. They were the headlamps of one of the half-tracks, waiting for them at the end of the line. The driver, Mark, was waiting there too.

Argen stopped the train with the engine but a few yards from the half-track. Mark came eagerly to meet them.

"Hello, Cliff, am I glad to see you! I was beginning to think the Meks had got you, after all. Bruce told me to wait here all night for you, if necessary. But where's Magnus?"

"Oh, he's here, safe enough – and sound asleep."

He was so sound asleep that it took both of them to awaken him. Mark was curious about the Mek, and became even more curious because Cliff hadn't time for a proper explanation then. They got Magnus, only partly awake, into the half-track.

Argen was still sleepy, too. Cliff, with his smattering of Bamu, managed to make him understand that they would give him a lift back to the ship, if he wished, or drop him off in the village. Argen conveyed that, for a change, he would like to see his own bed again, in his own house.

So Mark turned his vehicle around, and they drove slowly back to the village. The headlamps helped a bit but not much: the mist reflected their light confusingly. They dropped Argen at his house, and continued on to the ship. Magnus was already asleep again in the back of the truck. Cliff sat in front, beside Mark, the Mek on his lap like a large, sleeping child. Cliff used the time to relate the whole story to the interested Mark.

They had to awaken Magnus again at the gangplank, though he managed to climb it under his own steam. He muttered to Cliff: "I've never felt so utterly whacked before in my life."

Bruce and the Captain were waiting for them.

Magnus told Bruce wearily: "I'm afraid I've had it for to-night, Baldy. I'm going straight to bed. My young colleague here will put you in the picture, as you call it. But first, get the Doc to take a look at the Mek Manikin we've brought you back."

He reeled off.

The rest of them waited in the sick bay while the doctor examined the still insensible Mek. He removed the tunic, revealing the rather flabby white body.

"The bone formation is remarkably similar to ours," he said, feeling the arms and chest. "More delicate, though. Lack of sunlight doesn't encourage good bone growth on Venus."

"Nothing broken?" asked Bruce.

"I don't think so. It looks like a simple case of concussion, nothing more. I think he'll be coming round pretty soon."

"If he does, let us know," said Bruce, quietly. They tiptoed out, because Lamburn was asleep in the other bunk.

They went to Bruce's cabin for one of his beloved conferences.

117

But it wasn't the same without Magnus. Cliff wished he had been there to liven things up with a joke. Also, to make a better job of recounting what had happened in the Mek Forest. He stumbled through the recital somehow, while Beckworth Bruce and the Captain listened impassively. Bruce himself had had a hard day and looked older and more shrunken than ever.

At the end of it, Captain Browne said: "A most fantastic story! It's just like a dream!"

"Sometimes," said Bruce, with a sigh, "all life seems to me just like a dream. Is this any crazier than the Wooden Horse of Troy, or the Great Wall of China, or the Egyptian pyramids, or the witch-doctors of Central Africa, or the Children's Crusade, or the atomic war rockets of old, or a hundred other fantastic happenings on our own world? At least, there's reason behind this. The Meks used the giants as scarecrows to keep the bloodthirsty Bamus and their like out of the wood. Why should they go to the trouble of using direct force, when a mere myth could keep the peace for them? By employing psychological warfare only, they've conquered the Bamus and made them their slaves."

"But where do the Venusians fit into this?" asked the Captain. "Or don't they?"

Bruce hunched his shoulders, meaning that he didn't know, and began to fill his pipe.

The door opened and the doctor came into the room, leading the wide-eyed Mek by the hand. The Mek had a bandage round his head and looked dazed. He also looked pathetically small.

"I say, Doc," protested Captain Browne, "surely he's not well enough to be up and about already?"

The doctor looked a trifle hurt. "I gathered you wanted to try to pick up something of his language and question him, as you did with the Bamu last night. Frankly, I can't sanction such a cross-examination being carried on in the sick bay – not just now. It would disturb Lamburn, and he still needs all the sleep he can get. This fellow's only had a bang on the head. He'll be all right, if you don't bully him."

"You attend to your own business, doctor, and leave him to us," said Bruce, sharply. "And don't accuse us of bullying."

"I only meant –" began the doctor.

"Get back to your precious sick bay, doctor," said Bruce, in a distinctly bullying tone.

The doctor withdrew without another word, leaving the Mek standing there forlornly.

Cliff looked at Beckworth Bruce carefully. This was not the

real "Baldy", as he had know him. The old man was really tired and worried. He was being worn down by this endless tangle of mysteries, which seemed as if it would never be sorted out. He was responsible for establishing the Venus Base, and the more he tried to find solid ground for its foundation, the more unsure that ground became.

Doran didn't make many mistakes, but Cliff suspected now that he had made one here by over-estimating the remaining strength of the old hero. A younger, more resilient man should have been in charge of the Venus Expedition. The pace was a bit too hot – even Magnus had found it so.

Captain Browne, who concealed a tender heart behind a largely expressionless manner, was assisting the apprehensive little Mek into his own chair. The Mek sat there, his feet dangling off the floor, and looked shyly from one to another of them. Cliff smiled at him, wishing to encourage him. Whereupon the Mek promptly avoided his eyes.

"I wish Magnus were here," mumbled Bruce. "I was never much good at this sort of thing."

"Offer him a potato," said the Captain, with a rare attempt at humour, which Bruce ignored.

"Can I try?" asked Cliff, remembering Magnus's opening gambit with Argen the previous night. Bruce nodded, so Cliff began, pointing a finger at himself: "I – man. You – Mek?"

The Mek apparently found the floor more interesting than Cliff, and gazed fixedly at it. Nor could anything Cliff said make him raise his head. Presently, Cliff began to feel like a fool. He could sense Bruce's growing impatience and the Captain's silent amusement.

Bruce said, suddenly: "Magnus said something about making the first approach through the stomach. So let's try him with some food. Even if he throws it at us, at least it'll be *some* sort of reaction."

They sent for a dish of vegetables and held it under the Mek's resolutely downcast face. There was a reaction of a kind. The Mek picked up an onion, smelt it, then looked hard at them, as if he were asking them a question with his dark, sombre eyes. But they couldn't understand the question.

Cliff said, idiotically: "Food – munch – good. Munch – understand? You eat."

He put an imaginary onion in his mouth and chewed hard at nothing.

The Mek looked at him distastefully, and his gaze wandered

119

round the cabin. Obviously, he was looking for something and, equally obviously, he couldn't see it. He replaced the onion on the plate with care, and relapsed into shyness or indifference.

"Oh, to the devil with it!" exclaimed Bruce, irritably. "We'll have to wait until Magnus wakes up. I'd like to get to bed myself. The days may be short here, but they're confoundedly tiring. How about it, skipper?"

"I don't feel too bad," said Browne. "But I don't think I can be much help here – it's not in my line. I think I should check the stores with the quartermaster. We'll have to start rationing water, for one thing, if we're to supply the Bamus as well."

"Off you go, then," said Bruce. "See you in the morning."

The Captain went, glad to get away.

"Now, son," said Bruce to Cliff, "don't you feel like bed? Never mind the Mek laddie here – I'll put him back in the Doc's charge."

Cliff was on the point of giving in, when a sudden hot feeling of rebellion came over him. Why should they all be so condescending towards him, as though he were someone of small account – only Martin Magnus's sidekick? They all respected Magnus. They were content to wait all night for Magnus. Admittedly, they'd given him, Cliff, a chance, and so far he'd made nothing of it. But then, Magnus had had a tough time making any headway with Argen last night. But they'd allowed *him* to go on – they'd allowed him all night. It was only fair they should give the same chance to his fellow S.I.D. man – not dismiss him, however kindly, merely because he wasn't Martin Magnus.

He found himself saying: "I think, sir, if you'll give me the facilities Magnus had last night, I'll be able to show some useful results in the morning."

Bruce stared at him. "What facilities?"

Cliff gulped. "The use of your cabin, sir, and the tape recorder, and – er – privacy . . ."

"And my bed?" asked Bruce, dangerously.

Cliff could think of no suitably evasive answer.

"'Pon my word!" exclaimed Bruce, swivelling in his chair and addressing the ceiling. "Darn the boy – am I *never* to see my own bed again? Am I doomed for ever to sleep in the coalhole?"

He swung back again.

"All right," he said. "He's yours. My cabin is yours. My bed is yours. But unless you produce at the breakfast table a reasonable First Primer in Mekese, or whatever they call the confounded

120

language, then I'll see to it personally that you're hanged from the yard-arm."

He gave a sudden, ferocious, and apparently quite mirthless grin, stamped out, and banged the door behind him.

The temporary fire died in Cliff. He slumped back in his chair and a sick feeling crept into his stomach. He looked at the Mek, who sat stolidly regarding the floor as though he were waiting for it to do something.

"Gosh, what have I done now?" whispered Cliff to himself.

The door opened and the doctor came in. "Hello, where's everybody?"

"I'm here," said Cliff, dully defiant.

"Old Baldy wasn't in the best of moods, was he?"

"He's tired," said Cliff.

"Aren't we all? I think it's the low oxygen content in the atmosphere. I'll be the medical officer in the base, when it's started. I'm not looking forward to it much now. You're lucky. You'll be going back to Earth. How are you getting on with this chappie?"

"I'm not," said Cliff. "He ignores everything I say to him."

"I'm not surprised," said the doctor. "What can you hear if you haven't got ears?"

"Eh?" said Cliff, startled.

The doctor took a pace forward and gently lifted the Mek's head. He drew back the long black hair which Cliff had imagined covered the Mek's ears. Only – as it now became plain – there were no ears.

"I discovered that when I was bandaging him," said the doctor. "I was going to tell Bruce about it, but he gave me no chance. He flung me out – very rudely, don't you think?"

Cliff was dazed, and didn't answer.

"Oh, well," said the doctor. "There it is. No good talking to him. You'd better try sign language. Good night."

He went. Cliff and the Mek looked silently at each other. The Mek was expressionless, Cliff's expression became one of despair. He was telling himself: "Clifford Page, you're just a jealous fool! You've bitten off more than you can chew. And more than Magnus could chew. What do you do now?"

He looked the Mek up and down, at the silly little steel gaiters, the tight-fitting trousers, the black tunic which had been put on him again, the white, sharp little face with the black, soulful eyes, and the white bandage and the lank, dark hair. For the first time he noticed a breast pocket in the tunic, with a flap and a small button showing on it.

121

He reached out and attempted to undo the button. The Mek didn't resist. But the button wouldn't undo because, as he saw on closer inspection, there was no buttonhole.

"Buttons!" he said, aloud. "You Meks are button-mad!"

Then an idea struck him. He pressed the button, and the flap opened of itself. Gingerly, he felt the pocket. It contained something that felt like one of Magnus's cigars. He inserted his fingers and withdrew a thin, black rod. Shocked, he laid it on Bruce's desk, trying to take in this new discovery.

He had never seen the thought-rod which the Venusians of the lake had sent back to the Earthmen in Earth's own exploratory automatic scout-rocket. But Magnus had described it to him often enough. This, pretty certainly, was another like it. There was only one doubtful point. The Venusians' rod had been slightly slimy, because they left a thin layer of slime on everything they touched. But this one seemed to be quite dry.

He picked it up, prudently. He waited for thoughts to come into his mind from it, but none came. Perhaps he was mistaken, after all. But then, Magnus had learned from Argen that the Meks conveyed their wishes to the Bamus by this means. Why had none of them remembered that? Magnus and Bruce had been too tired, perhaps, and he – Cliff – had been too dull.

As he pondered, the rod was quietly taken from his fingers. He looked up, surprised. The Mek had reached for it, and there was interest in his round eyes.

The Mek held it for a short while, and returned it.

"What do you mean by that?" asked Cliff, puzzledly, forgetting the other's deafness.

There was no answer – at least, not in direct speech. But words crept into his mind. At first, they were his own – his earlier thoughts recorded: "A thought-rod, surely? But . . . no slime. And no thoughts. I must be mistaken. But Magnus said the Meks used thought-rods to convey their wishes to the Bamus. Why did none of us remember that? Perhaps Magnus and Bruce were too tired – and I was too dull."

And then thoughts that were not his own went on: "Yes, this is a thought-rod. This is how we communicate with each other, and how the Venusians communicate with us, and we to the Bamus. We are Mek Men. We make the machines for the Venusians. We do not design them ourselves. We only carry out the Venusians's orders. We build to their designs. We are clever with our hands but not with our brains. The Venusians have no hands. They cannot work metal under water. We are their hands. You must not interfere with us. You must not interfere with them. Their world is their world."

That was all. That was what the Mek Man had thought during the few moments he had held the rod.

Cliff sat back in his chair, shaken, amazed, and yet excited and almost happy because he had opened up a marvellous channel of communication when all hope of any interchange of ideas seemed futile. That the main point of the message was only a repetition of the earlier Venusian message, "Our world is our world", a deliberate handing off, seemed unimportant. There would be time to argue about that later.

He held the rod and thought again: "We are friends. We want nothing from this world but water. You supply it. Can we come to some arrangement?"

He proffered the rod and the Mek took it and held it for a few seconds while he absorbed the message. Then he took from an inside pocket of the tunic a metal ring, only slightly larger in diameter than the rod. Holding it between his long, delicate fingers, he passed it along the rod from end to end.

Afterwards, he held the rod briefly, obviously thinking, and returned it to Cliff. This time there was no repeating of the earlier thoughts and Cliff divined the purpose of the ring. It was to erase the clutter of previous thoughts and leave the rod free for current messages – much as speech impulses registered on magnetic tape could be erased and the tape used again.

The Mek's thoughts said directly: "We do not supply the water. It belongs to the Venusians. We do only what they tell us."

"Then we must communicate with them," replied Cliff, through the rod.

The answer came: "They want nothing to do with you. They do not want you on this planet. They want you to leave at once. They warned you even before you landed."

"Their world is their world," sighed Cliff, aloud. Despite the discovery of this ideal means of conversation, really getting anywhere with it didn't promise to be easy. He resigned himself to a long session, after all.

CHAPTER NINE

ULTIMATUM!

In the early morning the scene was reminiscent of that at the same time yesterday, save that a tired-eyed Cliff sat writing at the desk in place of Magnus when Bruce returned to the cabin from which he had been exiled.

Automatically, Bruce glanced at his bunk. There, as he had half expected, was the Mek curled up asleep in it.

He snorted. "I suppose tomorrow morning we'll have a full-grown Venusian jellyfish snoring away in my bed! I see you've got something down in writing there, Page, so I presume you got the Mek to talk."

"After a fashion."

"Did you get anything on the tape?" asked Bruce, switching the recorder on.

Cliff reached over and switched it off. "I didn't use this machine. I found another sort of recorder."

He held up the thought-rod, and explained to the surprised old man how it had been employed, adding that the Mek was deaf. He went on: "It wasn't easy to pump him. Frankly, he's a bit of a simpleton, and I think that goes for all the Meks. They're just the Venusians' stooges and general handymen – perhaps 'craftsmen' would be the better term."

"I see," said Bruce. "Well, we'll have the other two in for another of our pre-breakfast pow-wows. This seems to be becoming a regular thing."

Magnus didn't wait to be sent for. He came walking in a moment later, sprightly, his old self again. But the Captain had to be roused, for he had turned in late.

When they were all settled, Cliff read his report while Magnus watched him with a twinkle in his eye. He fully appreciated their reversed rôles on this occasion, and approved of it. His erstwhile protégé was emerging from his apprenticeship and becoming a real partner to him on equal terms.

Cliff explained the relationship between the Meks and the Venusians. The Meks did exactly as they were told, scrupulously.

124

"Too scrupulously, sometimes," said Cliff, smiling. "A long time ago the Venusians learned somehow – perhaps by radar – that Venus wasn't the only planet revolving round the Sun. I don't know if they discovered just how many there are. I rather doubt it. I think they could tell only vaguely that there was a planet between them and the Sun, and another outside their own orbit – their next-door neighbours on either side, as it were. They designed, and the Meks built, some sizeable spaceships to investigate these neighbours. But not in any spirit of scientific curiosity. They merely wanted to be sure no creatures lived there who might later bother them."

"You mean," said Magnus, "they wanted to learn if they had any neighbours they didn't want to speak to."

"That's it," grinned Cliff. "As they've now well and truly rubbed into us, they're extraordinarily jealous of their privacy. They sent the Meks to spy for them. Their job was to set up a base on each planet in turn, explore it thoroughly and report on it and its inhabitants, if any. They went to Mercury first. Of course, they found no life in the appalling extremes of temperature there. They reported back, and were instructed to do the same on the next planet in the other direction – outwards from the Sun. And they did."

"The Meks came to Earth?" frowned Bruce.

Cliff was still grinning. "No. They obeyed the Venusians' orders too scrupulously. It so happened that at the time they were nearing Earth, the Moon lay between Earth and Venus. So the Moon was in actual fact the next planet to Venus, and they landed there, quite ignoring Earth. I told you they were dim – and that they do exactly what the Venusians tell 'em, neither more nor less. They wouldn't dream of querying the instructions."

"I presume this was in the middle of the nineteenth century?" said Magnus. "When they roofed over Linné and made their base on the Moon?"

Cliff nodded. "Yes. Completing that base was a long job, not helped by there being no breathable atmosphere. It was a big job, too, as we know. And although they had marvellous machines to help them – which they had to ferry, often only one at a time, all the way from their workshops on Venus – they were only little folk, after all. Over a century passed before they'd finished their map and general survey of the Moon. Actually, time means little to them and less to the Venusians. Even after that, they'd missed finding the decapods – though only narrowly – and they never mentioned the existence of Earth."

125

"We found a fragment of their map in that midget submarine," remarked Magnus. "I suppose that was when they came closest to bumping into the decapods?"

"Yes," said Cliff. "It happened that the cave systems didn't quite connect up there. This was in the later days, when they were exploring the cave systems underground very thoroughly, having mapped the lunar surface. They used submarines quite a lot and lost more than one of them. But they were *not* midget subs., Magnus, nor robot ones, either. It was the Meks who were the midgets, and they manned them."

"Perhaps we're rather dim, too, for not guessing that," said Magnus.

"We guessed the size of their spaceships wrongly, too," said Cliff. "They were big, but not the colossal size we imagined. The Linné base was designed to accommodate five or six of them at once. And the spiral groove was a way of unloading them all at the same time.

"But what about those huge doorways we saw and thought were for giants to enter?"

"They were for the tall machines to go through," smiled Cliff. "But they may have been intended to mislead, also. For centuries the Meks had been playing a game of bluff of that kind with the natives here. It had become a habit with them. I suppose that's why, quite ridiculously, they took that collection of fake weapons with them to the Moon, in case there were any natives there they'd have to bluff. Naturally, there weren't, so when they quitted the base they just abandoned the weapons there."

"So," said Bruce, "they came back and reported to the Venusians that both their neighbouring planets were dead worlds?"

"Yes, they did," said Cliff. "Therefore, you can imagine that the Venusians were disturbed when they had a visit from our automatic scout-rocket. They couldn't understand where it had come from. So, not trusting the Meks to do the job this time, one of them followed the scout back himself – and discovered Earth and all its teeming life, and also what a conscientious bungle the Meks had made of their mission."

They all laughed, and looked over at the little Mek, still sound asleep in Bruce's bunk.

"They're curious folk," commented Cliff. "Quite single-minded in their service to the Venusians, and yet harmless – peace-loving, in fact, to the point of cowardice. They're in mortal terror, really, of the warring tribes who surround them. They

126

keep them busy digging and working, to stop them from hitting the war-path too often. Of course, they do use some of the mineral ore the tribes bring to them, but nothing like all of it. They're becoming embarrassed by the surplus, and are wondering where to store it."

"I expect we can use that when we get going here," said the Captain.

"We need water before that," said Bruce. "What's our chances, young man?"

Cliff said: "The water comes from the Venusians' lake which extends for miles underground, right to the heart of the Mek forest. It's piped from there. There's a stop-cock there. The Meks adjust it according to the Venusians' orders, which in turn depend on the ore supply reports submitted by the Meks. Actually, you see, it's the Venusians who have got both the Meks and the natives under their thumb. Our friend over there had come along on his stilts to check the load we'd just dumped. Also, to check that we'd left the forest. Hence, the giant get-up, to frighten us off if we were still lingering. When they're sure the coast is clear, the Meks run a train from their city in the centre of the wood to pick up the load –"

"The water," Bruce reminded him, impatiently.

"The Mek says it's solely the Venusians' affair. And as the Venusians refuse to discuss it with us, the Mek says he can do – and will do – nothing to help us."

"Then we'll make him," said Magnus, suddenly.

"How?" asked the Captain, rounding on him. "I draw the line at any form of torture –"

"Tush!" said Magnus. "I'll be back in a few minutes."

He left the cabin.

"It'll be difficult to use force on the Venusians, tucked away in their lake," said Bruce, frowning. "The 'vibes' won't affect those jellyfish – we discovered that when we tried it back on Earth. We haven't any atomic bombs. Anyway, if we had, and used them in the lake, the water would become so radio-active it would be useless to us. What about ordinary high-explosive bombs? We could make them and throw them in –"

"If we could get near the lake," said Cliff. "But you know what happened to Magnus and me there."

"Supposing this time you were wearing the spacesuits?"

Cliff shook his head. "No use, sir. That acid gas they use eats metal away as though it were cheese."

"Right, then," said Bruce, not to be defeated. "We've a heli-

127

copter stored in parts aboard ship. We'll assemble it, fly over the lake out of range of the gas, and *drop* the darned bombs on them if they refuse to co-operate."

"I don't approve of murder," said the Captain, distantly.

Again, Cliff shook his head. "That gun they have – which is the only one, so far as I know – happens to be an anti-aircraft gun, radar-directed, at that. They've a pile of shells, all fitted with proximity fuses. They could shoot us down before we got anywhere near them."

"Anti-aircraft gun?" echoed Bruce, as Magnus re-entered.

"My brother made a special study of such guns – he's interested in the history of artillery," said Cliff, not too happily.

"What's that got to do with it?"

"Well, sir, as you know, that single Venusian searched his mind somehow. I believe now it must have been done using this thought-rod medium in some fashion. One's thoughts just cling to the stuff, and if they're not erased, they accumulate. To some extent it worked the other way round, for Ken learned some of the Venusian's private thoughts. But it must have learned a great deal more of his. He was in a trance-like state, his mind wandering, and probably something of this gunnery stuff floated to the surface at some time or another. I think – and hope – it was only the anti-aircraft side of it. So far as I gathered from the Mek, the Venusians have only understood the idea of shooting at aerial targets. Which was why the ship was shelled only in the air. They were warning us off, with a deliberate near-miss. So long as the ship remains grounded, though, it's probably safe from the gun. Proximity fuses are pretty useless for field gunnery, anyway."

"Nevertheless," said Magnus, "we'd better find that gun and destroy it."

"By the Venusians' orders the Meks set it up beside the lake," said Cliff. "They fire it by remote control from there. So how do we get at it to destroy it? We'd be destroyed first."

"Taking it all round, then, the Venusians have the whip hand," said Bruce. He scratched his shining pate and sighed. "I'm darned if I can see a way to get on top of them. We're stymied. Let's leave it for a bit and have breakfast. Do you think your Mek friend will join us this time?"

"I'm sure I don't know," Cliff answered. "I'll waken him."

Once again, breakfast was a curious meal. The little Mek sat in the chair which the tall Argen had occupied yesterday. He seemed shy again in the presence of all of them, When Cliff tried to communicate with him via the thought-rod, he refused to take it. He

128

refused to take any breakfast, either, and sat looking down solemnly at the plate of cereal placed before him.

"Not exactly a sparkling conversationalist, is he?" remarked Bruce.

But when the bacon and eggs were brought in, together with the cruet, the Mek's eyes lit up. He snatched the salt cellar and emptied its entire contents over his cereal, mixed it well in, and began eating the salt-smothered shreds with avidity.

All except Magnus watched him with astonishment.

"I've seen natives do that along the Congo," said Magnus. "They love salt so much they'll eat it by itself, in handfuls."

"Well, now we know what he was looking for to go with the onion, last night," said the Captain. "Good heavens, what's that? Are we being attacked?"

He started up, like the others, except Magnus, and except the Mek, who couldn't hear the terrible screaming and shouting which had started up suddenly somewhere just outside the ship.

They crowded to the porthole. There, below, the entire male population of the village had turned out, their faces and limbs hideously painted with purple dye. They were dancing wildly around, sometimes to steps, sometimes not, brandishing spears and bows and yelling their heads off. Argen was out in front, performing a mad solo.

"Don't worry, it's only their traditional war dance – by special request," said Magnus, still at the table, pouring a second cup of tea.

"*Your* request, I suppose?" said Bruce, over his shoulder.

Magnus nodded, drank the tea at a gulp, and said: "Yes, I sent a message to Argen to organize it at short notice."

"Why?" asked the Captain.

"I'll show you," said Magnus. He rose, grabbed the unsuspecting Mek under the armpits, carried him over to the porthole and held him up there. The Mek took one horrified look at the spectacle, then turned his head away and struggled to free himself. Magnus set him down.

"Quiet, now, folks," he said. He had brought the thought-rod with him, and after a few moments' concentration on it he held it out to the shrinking Mek, who refused to take it. Magnus pointed to the porthole, threateningly, and proffered the rod again.

This time the Mek took it. They handed it to each other several times in silence, while the others watched.

"All right," said Magnus, finally. "He's going to show us how to contact the Venusians. I told him if he didn't, we should give the Meks' secret away to the Bamus – tell 'em the Meks aren't really giants at all, but only frightened little men. And then the Bamus and all the other tribes would overrun the forest and kill them all. And the Venusians would lose their artificers, and it would be a bad show all round. That, and the sight of what the Bamus look like on the war-path, finished him. I suggest that Cliff and I go with him directly I've stopped that hullabaloo outside."

"You'd better take a party with you –" began Bruce, but Magnus cut in: "Don't let's go all over that again, Baldy. Just leave it to the Special Investigation Department – we can handle it. We've got our 'vibes' – they'll stop the Meks if they try anything, and I don't think they will. They'll be too scared of the rest of you setting the Bamus on to them in reprisal. Now I must tell Argen it's time to break up the party, though it's a howling success, don't you think?"

*

The little locomotive, driven by Magnus, and pulling only one truck, which contained Cliff and the Mek, rolled on into the forest, past the point where the broken ends of the trip wire still lay, although the fallen legs had been removed. On down the avenue it went, between the great-girthed trees, under the canopy of mist.

They were not bound for Mek City, which Cliff had gathered lay somewhere underground in the heart of the forest, lit by that same mysterious light which they had encountered in the Linné base. For, as he'd also learned, the Meks' eyesight was no better than their own, and they could see only dimly in the forest. It came as a shock to the Mek when Cliff informed him that the Bamus could see quite well through the mist, and it was pure chance that they hadn't literally seen through the trick of the bogus giant long before this. Cliff suggested that in future the Meks should build complete mechanical giants.

Exploration of Mek City would have to come later in the programme. It was a side issue compared with tackling the Venusians. And they could be contacted only at one point in the forest, well away from the city.

Presently, the avenue branched and the railway lines branched with it. The Mek showed them how to move the points, and the short train turned off the direct track and went gliding on down a somewhat narrower avenue. The forest was as quiet as ever and nothing and no one but themselves appeared to be moving in it.

Cliff had charge of a powerful two-way radio they'd set up in the truck, netted to the ship's set, and from time to time he reported their progress to Bruce.

Then the train ran into a cutting, driving deeper into the hill. Presently, they saw the mouth of a lighted tunnel ahead. They were expecting this, because the Mek had told them they would have to go underground. The walls of the tunnel were smooth and bare and emitted clear white light.

It was shorter than they had anticipated, and came to a dead end in a long chamber which was about twice as wide and high as the tunnel. On one side were two doors, similar in pattern to the one at the bottom of the spiral groove in Linné.

Magnus stopped the locomotive neatly beside them, vaulted out, and then hesitated between them.

"Eeny, meeny, miny, mo," he said, waving a forefinger, and then set it on the button of the left-hand door. The door slid silently up into its hollow lintel, revealing a box-like compartment which was clearly a lift, and as clearly not a passenger one. It was full of tall metal containers on wheels. Magnus peered into one. It was empty save for a thin encrustation of white powder. He scooped up a little of the powder and smelt it. Then, cautiously, he licked one finger-tip – and pulled a wry face.

"Salt," he said.

The Mek had opened the other door, disclosing another lift, smaller, cleaner, and quite empty. The walls glowed with their own pale light.

"Ah – the first-class passenger lift," said Magnus.

Cliff didn't hear him. He was pressing his earphones tightly against his ears, straining to hear Bruce. Reception was bad below ground. Then he said into his microphone: "Can only just hear you. Strength One. Report my signals. Over."

It seemed that Bruce, through the powerful amplification of the ship's set, could hear him perfectly.

Magnus tapped Cliff on the shoulder. "Tell him we're closing down for a while to go down and explore the bargain basement."

Cliff complied, got the acknowledgment, switched off, and hung up the earphones.

The Mek was in the smaller lift, waiting for them. They entered, stooping, for the lift had been designed for people only half their height. The Mek did some expert button work, the door closed, and the lift began to sink.

Cliff said: "I hope we know what we're doing."

Magnus just smiled, looking pointedly at Cliff's hand resting on his vibrator.

The elevator was falling uncomfortably fast now, and it was obvious that the shaft was deep. At last it began to slow, then stopped, and a door rolled up in front of them. They stepped out, following the Mek, and found themselves in another chamber, much larger than the one up above. Indeed, one end of it widened out like a huge funnel. They stopped, staring along it, for it looked odd.

Just where the funnel began to open out, the walls seemed to lose their glowing internal light and became flat white, very bright, almost dazzling at first. But it was only reflected light, and weakened with distance until at last the walls faded away into ever-darkening shadow.

Running down the centre of the chamber, straight into that shadow, was another set of railway lines. A short way along it stood an empty train, on the same scale as the one they had used above ground.

"All change here," said Magnus. He started towards the train, but the Mek stopped him with a hasty gesture. He pointed at a closed door in the opposite wall of the chamber, and handed Magnus the thought-rod.

Magnus relayed the message verbally, "We're to wait here, Cliff. There are a couple of other Meks beyond the door, on some sort of duty, and our pal doesn't want us to go busting in right away and scare them. He wants to prepare them for the shock of our ugly mugs and explain why we're here."

"I suppose it's all right?" said Cliff, dubiously.

Magnus shrugged. "I don't think we've much to fear from the Meks. They know their game will be up if they play us false."

In a moment, he handed the rod back to the Mek, who took it expressionlessly and went through the doorway. They had a glimpse of a short passage before the door descended behind him, and that was all.

Magnus was curious about the flat walls and walked down the chamber to look at them. He picked tentatively at one wall, then went on towards the darkness. He probed about in that with his torch-beam.

Then to Cliff's relief, he went no farther, and returned.

"It's a salt mine," he reported. "And a pretty big one, so far as I could see. The Meks are sure fond of the cruet. They bring the stuff out in train loads, I suppose, and take it up in that lift. No wonder water's short on this planet – the Meks must raise such a thirst that they drink it all!"

"I wonder how many Meks there are?"

132

"Quite a number, I should imagine," said Magnus. "Ah, here's Micky back again."

It hadn't taken long for Magnus to pin the name "Micky the Mek Man" on their captive, who was now motioning them to come through the door. They followed him. The short passage led to a small room where two other Meks, looking exactly like "Micky", were pretending to study the dials on a control panel almost filling one end wall, but were really shyly watching the two Earthmen they'd just been told about.

Apart from them and the panel, which presumably was a contact with Mek City, the room was pretty bare. There was a bench and a couple of chairs, of stone or plastic, on a kindergarten scale. But what caught the eye at once were two large pipes, of what looked to be stainless steel, standing like pillars between floor and ceiling. One was about a yard in diameter. Its slimmer companion was only a quarter as wide. Each bore, like a growth on its side, a large spoked wheel controlling the stop cock.

The Mek ran his erasing ring over the thought rod, imprinted a message, and passed the rod to Magnus.

Magnus enlightened Cliff. "They're the water mains leading down from the Venusians' lake, which is just overhead here. The larger one supplies Mek City and is functioning. The secondary one runs underground to the pool in Lomba, and the stopcock is closed – at the moment. But we can soon remedy that."

He set both hands on the smaller wheel. Agitatedly, "Micky" seized his arm and pointed to a corner of the room. They took a second and closer look there at what, at first sight, had appeared merely to be a sort of washbowl, on a cylindrical base, with a couple of faucets jutting at an angle over it. Now they saw that the bowl itself was actually a closely woven wire mesh. And the faucets were bare, thin pipes, open ended but lacking taps.

The Mek conveyed another message.

"We mustn't turn the water on unless the Venusians agree to it," reported Magnus, slowly. "We can contact them through that washbasin contraption."

"But how?" asked Cliff.

As if the Mek had heard, he drew them across to the bowl and tapped a container on the side of its pedestal. Magnus looked into it. The container was full of thought-rods, neatly, but loosely, packed. The Mek withdrew one, made a pretence of thinking a message on to it, and indicated that it was then to be stuffed up the right hand faucet. He handed the rod to Magnus, and motioned him to go ahead with it.

133

"I see," said Magnus. "It's really quite an old idea, Cliff – the pneumatic dispatch tubes, worked by compressed air. Why, they still use them for inter-office written memos in the S.I.D. building. Now, how do we address the Venusians? 'Dear Sirs ...'?"

He held the rod for some time, thinking.

"Give them my regards," said Cliff, presently.

Frowning, Magnus pushed the tube up the mouth of the narrow pipe, which it only just fitted. Before it was halfway through, an invisible force sucked it from his fingers and it vanished up the pipe.

Magnus said: "I've told them why we want water, that it's stupid of them to tell us to go home when we can't take off without water, that we have no intention of leaving Venus for good, in any case, and if they don't give us permission to turn the water on, we'll do it anyway."

"That'll give them something to chew on," said Cliff.

But the Venusians didn't chew on it for long. A couple of minutes later, a stream of water gushed from the other small pipe into the bowl, gurgling away through the mesh. The thought-rod came rattling out with it. The mesh stopped it. It lay there in the bowl with the water pouring over it. Then the column of water thinned, shrank to a trickle, and suddenly ceased to be.

Magnus picked up the wet rod gingerly.

"Ugh!" he exclaimed. "It's slimy. Of course – they've touched it."

The three Meks and Cliff watched him in silence as he absorbed the Venusians' reply.

Presently, he said: "They still don't like us, Cliff. They say we've no right to be on Venus. It's our own fault if we can't leave – we shouldn't have come in the first place. We have a world of our own, so why didn't we stay there? So now we can stay here on this one – and die of thirst, for they won't supply Lomba with any more water until we're all dead. Probably the Bamus will be dead by then, too, but the Venusians say they don't care about that: they have enough reserve of iron ore to last them indefinitely, and the Bamus were always troublesome, anyway."

"They couldn't have put it more plainly," said Cliff, bitterly. "But we can get the water, just the same.

He started towards the stop-cock.

"No!" exclaimed Magnus. "Don't touch it. They've got us there, too. They said if we open it, they'll play their old trick of changing the water into acid. We'll only succeed in pumping acid

134

into the metal pool, eating it away and ruining the whole pipe-line as well."

"The devils!" said Cliff, savagely. "Then we'll raid Mek City –"

"They're even prepared to sacrifice the Meks to defeat us," Magnus cut in quietly.

Cliff felt as though his head were whirling.

"What *can* we do, then? Radio Doran and ask him to send a rescue ship?"

"Talk sense, Cliff. There isn't another ship like *Archimedes II* in existence, nothing that could land here. We'd have to wait for them to build another, and then wait again for it to travel here. By that time we should be good and dead."

"Then it's hopeless. There isn't a thing we can do. We've considered every possible way of getting at the Venusians, but they have the answer every time. They're beyond our reach. We've got to face it, Magnus – our Venus colony is doomed before it's really got started."

"You disappoint me, son. I thought you'd made the grade. That's no way for an S.I.D. man to talk."

"I know. I'm sorry," said Cliff, ashamed but despairing. "But – there's just no way out."

"There's always a way out," said Magnus. "Remember that, always – else you don't belong in the S.I.D. Now, we'll start with a little diplomacy . . ."

He dropped the slimy thought-rod back into the bowl and selected a fresh one. In a few moments, he handed it to "Micky", whose dull face brightened. The Mek opened the door for them to leave.

"Where now?" asked Cliff.

"I've complimented him on the salt mine. Told him it looks bigger than any on Earth, which is rubbish, of course. He's going to show us over it."

"And what good will that do us?"

"I'm not sure yet – we'll see."

The Mek conducted them to the train outside, and while they were climbing in, touched hardly noticeable buttons on the wall. The floor leading into the dark mine became a gleaming strip, dwindling into the distance, casting light on all sides. They rode along it in the train, staring around at the far-spreading cavern with its walls of pure salt throwing back the light that arose from below them.

135

Magnus pointed to motionless machines, with great scoops, standing here and there beside the walls.

"They don't use Bamu labour here," he said. "There are the slaves who dig for them in this mine."

The cavern went on for three or four miles. At last they reached the end of it, and the train stopped. The Mek turned round in his cockpit, looking at them as though he expected them to break into applause.

"I think it's big enough," said Magnus, thoughtfully. "It'll do."

"It's terrific," Cliff admitted. "Thousands and thousands of tons of salt. Heaven knows how much they've already dug out. Surely they couldn't have eaten all that?"

"They don't take it a pinch at a time," smiled Magnus. "Anyhow, this mine has probably been in operation for hundreds of years." He passed the thought-rod to the Mek. "I'm telling him we agree it's terrific."

The Mek looked pleased, then reversed the train. When they arrived back in the chamber, Magnus exchanged more thoughts with the Mek, and then said to Cliff with a wink: "I've kidded him on about it. I've told him we're so impressed we'd like to take some measurements of the mine, and he's tickled pink. He's taking me up in the lift to collect our measuring tape."

"What?" said Cliff, dazed. "We didn't bring one."

"Yes, we did. I had it stowed in the cockpit of the other train. Didn't you notice? Anyhow, wait here – we shan't be long."

Still completely at sea, Cliff waited in the chamber while Magnus vanished into the passenger lift with "Micky". It wasn't good to have to wait there alone, for he began to think too much about the spot they were in. About Bruce, and Captain Browne, and the ship's crew, and the band of would-be colonists, and Doran, millions of miles away, all waiting for good news from Magnus and him – and all doomed to disappointment at best, and slow death for most of them at worst.

It seemed hours before the lift door opened again. "Micky" emerged, followed by Martin Magnus, who had the measuring tape with him: two reels of it. Only, Cliff knew it better by the name of "blasting tape". At once, his spirits lifted. It was plain that Magnus had a plan, and Magnus's plans usually worked. He tried not to look too excited.

"Help me lay it out," said Magnus. "We start here, at the door – and we lay it double."

They laid the lengths of the tape along by the wall, a bare inch apart, black side uppermost. They went on to the full extent of it, hugging the wall all the way. The Mek watched with interest, and brought his two fellows out to watch also.

"What's the idea?" whispered Cliff, as they worked. He needn't have bothered to whisper, for the Meks hadn't grown any ears lately.

Magnus said: "Surely you remember the tape-recording of Ken we have, taken when he was repeating the Venusian's thoughts in his sleep? We've played it over often enough. Remember that bit which runs: 'The water stings and stings unbearably'?"

"Yes," said Cliff, puzzledly. "Being fresh-water creatures, the Venusian found our sea water unbearable because – because of the salt in it! Gosh, now I see what your game is! You're going to bluff 'em by –"

"I'm not going to bluff anybody," said Magnus, soberly. "There, that's the end of it. We saw what this same amount of tape did at the mineral workings. If we set it off here, it'll blow the whole wall down. If the wall comes down, the bottom of this end of the lake will drop out. And the water will flood the whole mine, all those miles of it. It'll find its own level, of course, and the Venusians will survive. But they won't be able to stop thousands of tons of salt from dissolving away in their water. It'll sting 'em till they scream for mercy. It may seem drastic, but remember – they've shown no mercy to us."

Cliff looked at Magnus's grim expression and the chin that jutted like a spur of rock, and was silent. He wanted to know how they could get out of it alive themselves, and if they could and did, what use the salt water would be to them. Though, he supposed, by a slow process of boiling and condensing they could use some of it.

Magnus strode back to the little room, the Meks scurrying after him like children. Cliff followed hastily, too, and found Magnus standing by the bowl and checking the small pocket radio which transmitted the deadly frequencies.

"There's a delayed-action mechanism on this thing, you know," said Magnus. "We can set it, leave it here, take the express lift, and probably get out of the tunnel in the train before the zero second."

"If it should come to that," said Cliff, hesitantly, "we'll take the Meks with us, out of danger."

"Of course. Even if we have to 'vibe' them first."

He slipped the thin case back in his pocket and selected a rod

137

from the container. He held it for a moment, then passed it to "Micky" with a bland smile. He confided to Cliff: "I've asked him to describe, for the Venusians, how impressed we are with the salt mine and how we've been 'measuring' it. Poor Micky – he feels flattered!"

"I don't get it."

"It'll confirm what we've done," said Magnus. "Now I'll add the rest."

He took the rod back from the Mek, still with a gracious smile. But the smile died on his lips as mentally he composed a long message for the Venusians. Then he slid the rod into the appropriate pipe, and at once it was whisked away.

"There goes our ultimatum," he said, "and it's a stiff one. I've explained the power of B.T., and told them there's a practical example of it at the diggings if they care to check up on it. Perhaps they already know about that. If not, then it's too bad, for I've given them only ten minutes. First they're to fill their mountain bowl with acid gas, the way they did when we were there."

"Why?" asked Cliff, curiously.

"Because we daren't go near that gun, beside the lake, to destroy it. So we must force them to destroy it themselves. The gas will do that. Second, and more important, they must agree to supply Lomba with fresh water until such time as we can find our own supply on Venus. If they don't agree to these terms, then it's a nice strong brine bath for them. I've told them I mean it – and I do mean it."

"I can see you do," said Cliff.

There was nothing to do now but wait, and as the minutes ticked by Cliff began to pace up and down nervously. Magnus smiled and offered his cigar case. They both lit up long, thin cigars, to the wonderment of the patiently watching Meks.

And then water flowed from the left-hand pipe and a thought-rod rattled in the bowl.

"There's the answer," said Magnus.

They stood regarding it. Cliff was the nearer. He looked inquiringly at Magnus.

"Go ahead," said Magnus. "You read it."

Cliff picked up the slimy thing which meant life or death to them. His fingers trembled visibly. He gripped it, between repugnance and a burning curiosity. His mind was so tense that it formed a barrier to the thoughts reposing in the rod. He tried to relax, to think of nothing at all. And then the message came slowly to him in its entirety, for it consisted only of two words: "*We agree.*"

"They agree," he said, numbly, and then suddenly flung the rod across the room with a whoop. The Meks skipped hastily out of the way.

Magnus grinned round his cigar and seized the wheel of the smaller stop-cock.

"Aye, aye, sir – two points to starb'd," he said, and hauled on the wheel until the cock was fully open.

"Micky" eyed him doubtfully, then picked up the thought-rod from the floor and held it. The brief message from the Venusians dispelled his doubts.

He came up in the lift with them to the train. Cliff switched on the big radio set and contacted Bruce, who in turn was also in touch by walkie-talkie with a guard post in the village square.

"It's all right, Magnus," Cliff reported. "The pool is filling up fast – with cool, clear water."

"Mission completed," said Magnus, climbing into the driving cockpit. "Return to base. And soon it will be a real base – Venus Base Number One."

He motioned "Micky" to get in the truck with Cliff, but the Mek slipped him a thought-rod instead.

Magnus laughed when he read the message. "Micky's got to stay here because he's the next on duty down below," he said. "Well, so long, Micky – we'll probably meet up again sometime."

He started the engine, and the little train began to carry them along the lighted tunnel, towards the dimmer light of day outside. Yet, as they emerged into it, somehow it seemed a brighter day than when they had left it to enter the tunnel. Perhaps that was because now it held a much brighter promise.

EXCITING STORIES BY
ENID BLYTON

There are eleven thrilling "Mystery" books by Enid Blyton all in the Dragon series, and all waiting for you to read. Eleven delightful stories of our young detectives, the Five Find-outers, and of course Buster, the Scottie.

But also in Dragon editions are two wonderful school series by Enid Blyton. The first is the celebrated Malory Towers' series, which concerns Darrell Rivers and her friends, and what fun and adventures they have! What tricks they play on their French mistress, poor Mam'zelle, who never knows what the girls will be up to next. Six books about Malory Towers school, just waiting to give you hours of delicious reading. Look out for the first in the series – *First Term at Malory Towers*. You will enjoy it!

The other school series is about St. Clare's, about the O'Sullivan twins who are also full of fun, but having their share of adventure, too. When you have read the Mystery stories, and all the Malory Towers' books, you will want to read about the twins at St. Clares. Don't forget them!

PONY BOOKS

Do you like pony books? Have you ever tried them? They can be wonderfully exciting, and pony books now have tremendous sales among young people. In fact, after Enid Blyton stories, we sell more books about ponies than on any other subject.

In the Dragon series we have some wonderful pony books. Possibly the most loved is the story of Flicka. This appears in eight volumes – a magnificently long story – and the opening book is called *My Friend Flicka Part I*.

It is the story of a ranch in Wyoming, and of a boy who is given a pony. But that pony is a descendant of the wild horses that roam the range, and this brings heart-ache to the young owner; for Flicka is intractable for a long time and will not show affection.

The story–which has been read by millions all round the world – tells of the life of the wild horses: of summers that are happy for them, out there in the sun-lit mountains; of winters that are cruelly harsh. It also tells absorbingly of the life of the roaming herds of wild horses, of the fights by stallions to win the leadership of these herds for themselves. The Flicka books are exciting, heartwarming, and often they will move you to tears. Do decide now to buy the first of the Flicka series next time you go to your bookshop or newsagent.

Another series about horses in Dragon books is about the brumbies (wild horses) of Australia. There are four in this series, the first being entitled *The Silver Brumby*.

Again we have a pony series which might be described as a classic. Again we live with wild horses, with most men's hands turned against them, only wanting to be free and to be allowed to roam the wild wide acres without molestation.

Finally, we have excellent pony books by Gillian Baxter and Christine Pullein-Thompson. Delightful stories which have been big-selling for months. Why not start to collect your own pony library? At half-a-crown each the books are not expensive and in very little time you would have a bright array of titles you could be proud of. Make a resolution to buy a Dragon pony book a week!

DRAGON BOOKS

Thousands of children buy a Dragon book every week. *Why don't you?* Think of it, in no time what a wonderful library you would have, all of your very own. How gay those Dragon books on your bedroom shelf, favourites to read and re-read again and again. Ask your mum or dad if you can order a Dragon book every week from your bookseller or newsagent. After all, it's only half-a-crown. If you have difficulty in getting titles, they are obtainable from: Cash Sales Dept., P.O. Box 11, Falmouth, Cornwall, at the price shown plus 9d. postage.

All at 2/6 (unless shown)

Green Dragons

Pony Books

By Mary O'Hara

My Friend Flicka Part 1
My Friend Flicka Part 2
Thunderhead Part 1
Thunderhead Part 2

Thunderhead Part 3
Green Grass of Wyoming Part 1
Green Grass of Wyoming Part 2
Green Grass of Wyoming Part 3

The above are all books about Flicka in order of appearance

By Gillian Baxter

Jump to the Stars
The Difficult Summer
The Perfect Horse

Tan and Tarmac
Horses in the Glen
Ribbons and Rings

By Christine Pullein-Thompson

The First Rosette
The Second Mount
Three to Ride

The Empty Field
The Open Gate
The Pony Dopers

By Elyne Mitchell

The Silver Brumby   3/6
Silver Brumby's Daughter   3/6

Silver Brumbies of the South
Silver Brumby Kingdom

Adventure Stories

By William F. Temple

Martin Magnus, Planet-Rover 3/6   Martin Magnus on Venus   3/6

By Arthur Catherall

Ten Fathoms Deep
Jackals of the Sea

Forgotten Submarine
Sea Wolves

By Showell Styles

Midshipman Quinn
Quinn of the Fury
The Shop in the Mountain

The Ladder of Snow
A Necklace of Glaciers
The Pass of Morning

By David Scott Daniell

Mission for Oliver
Polly and Oliver

Polly and Oliver Besieged

By Edgar Rice Burroughs

Tarzan of the Apes
The Return of Tarzan
The Beasts of Tarzan
Tarzan and the Ant-Men

Tarzan's Quest
The Warlord of Mars
Thuvia, Maid of Mars

The House in Cornwall
Adventure in Forgotten Valley
The Mysterious Rocket
Dolphin Island
An Edge of the Forest
Australian Adventure
The Three Musketeers

Noel Streatfeild
Glyn Frewer
André Massepain
Arthur C. Clarke
Agnes Smith
Maria Wolkowsky
Alexander Dumas

All at 3/6 (unless shown)

Red Dragons   **By Enid Blyton**

Mystery of The Burnt Cottage
Mystery of The Disappearing Cat
Mystery of The Secret Room
Mystery of The Hidden House
Mystery of The Spiteful Letters
Mystery of The Pantomime Cat
Mystery of The Missing Necklace
Mystery of The Invisible Thief
Mystery of The Vanished Prince
Mystery of The Strange Bundle
Mystery of Holly Lane
Mystery of The Strange Messages
Mystery of Tally-ho Cottage

First Term at Malory Towers
Second Form at Malory Towers
Third Year at Malory Towers
Upper Fourth at Malory Towers
In The Fifth at Malory Towers
Last Term at Mallory Towers
The O'Sullivan Twins
The Twins at St. Clare's
Summer Term at St. Clare's
Second Form at St. Clare's
Claudine at St. Clare's
Fifth Formers at St. Clare's
Mystery of The Missing Man

Mystery of Banshee Towers

The Coral Island 2/6
Knights of the Cardboard Castle   2/6

R. M. Ballantyne
Elisabeth Beresford

Blue Dragons   **By Enid Blyton**

The Red Story Book   2/6
The Blue Story Book   2/6

The Yellow Story Book   2/6
The Green Story Book   2/6

Eight O'Clock Tales   2/6